"Silent Souls"
and Other Stories

CATERINA ALBERT

"Silent Souls" and Other Stories

Translated by Kathleen McNerney

The Modern Language Association of America
New York   2018

© 2018 by The Modern Language Association of America
All rights reserved
Printed in the United States of America

MLA and the MODERN LANGUAGE ASSOCIATION are trademarks
owned by the Modern Language Association of America. For information
about obtaining permission to reprint material from MLA book
publications, send your request by mail (see address below) or
e-mail (permissions@mla.org).

Library of Congress Cataloging-in-Publication Data is available
from the Library of Congress.

ISSN: 1079-2538

Cover illustration of the paperback and electronic editions:
Photograph, by Benjamin Bofarull Gallofré, in the Víctor Català Archive,
of *L'Escala* or *View from Punta Montgó*, a painting by Caterina Albert.

Published by The Modern Language Association of America
85 Broad Street, suite 500, New York, New York 10004-2434
www.mla.org

To Francesca Bartrina,
in memoriam

CONTENTS

ACKNOWLEDGMENTS

While I consider my ten-week stay in the lovely birthplace of Caterina Albert a gift from the goddesses, there are a number of down-to-earth organizations and individuals to thank as well. West Virginia University allowed me to take a sabbatical year, and the Cultural Department of the Ajuntament (City Hall) of L'Escala awarded me a grant and a lovely modernist house overlooking the Mediterranean in the fifteenth-century village of Sant Martí d'Empúries. Pere Guanter, head of the Cultural Department, and his entire team at City Hall aided me in many ways during my stay. Several experts in translation and on the work of Albert were also extremely helpful, especially Francesca Bartrina, Ron Puppo, and Teresa Vall, who gave close readings to several difficult passages, making suggestions or simply explaining various meanings. Núria Nardi and Irene Muñoz lent a hand with bibliographic items, and all the above-named people went beyond professionalism to visit or take me out when a break was in order. The people of the village of Sant Martí were most friendly and gracious. Anna Sánchez Rue and María Gutiérrez in Barcelona, Maria-Antònia Oliver in Mallorca, and Carles Cortés and Zequi Moltó in Alacant offered me their hospitality and a constant helping hand.

Acknowledgments

On this side of the Atlantic, my longtime friends Judith Stitzel and Anna Elfenbein gave me positive suggestions for the introduction, and Susana Villanueva Eguía Lis helped with all manner of technical matters. Special thanks to the Albert family in L'Escala.

INTRODUCTION

Reading and understanding Catalan literature present a series of questions, as much for professors as for students of His panic literatures and cultures. When we read a text from the Hispanic world, one of the first questions we ask is, From what part of this vast world does the text emerge? If we narrow the place down to the Iberian Peninsula and the Balearic and Canary Islands, our quest cannot stop there, because we know that this area speaks, thinks, and writes not in one language but several: Portuguese, Galician, Castilian, Euskera, and Catalan. Some might add even others, such as Bable, or all the African languages spoken in the former colonies of Portugal and Spain. The study of the literatures written in these languages raises difficult and fascinating questions having to do with the concepts of nation, national consciousness, and national literature.[1]

Caterina Albert i Paradís (1869–1966) wrote most of her work in Catalan, the language of many writers who are included in the Spanish literary canon or, more precisely, the literary canon of Iberia. Among the major figures writing in Catalan are Ramon Llull (1235–1315), a medieval thinker and mystic who influenced many subsequent philosophers, including Gottfried Wilhelm Leibniz; Ausias March (1397–1459), a cultivator of Petrarchan poetry who had a lasting effect on

Spanish verse; Joanot Martorell (1413–68), whose *Tirant lo Blanch* was saved from Miguel de Cervantes's book-burning scene in *Don Quixote*; and, in the twentieth century, Mercè Rodoreda (1908–83), author of *La Plaça del Diamant* (in Spanish, *Plaza del Diamante*; in English, *Time of the Doves*), one of the most riveting re-creations of life during the Spanish Civil War. Albert has much in common with her contemporaries Anton Chekhov and Emilia Pardo Bazán: she shares many narrative techniques with them as well as an intense interest in the psychological development of characters. Yet she is widely read only in Catalonia. That she is little known outside Catalonia is the result not only of the vagaries of literary taste or the market but also of the history of the Catalan language and the history of Catalonia in the Spanish state.

A first step toward understanding the work of Albert is to situate it in the context of Catalan, Spanish, and European culture of the late nineteenth century and well into the twentieth. She first came to the attention of the Catalan literary world in 1898, when in the small northern town of Olot she entered two of the traditional literary contests known as the Jocs Florals ("Floral Games"). She won both. The Jocs Florals flourished in France and Spain in the fourteenth century but ceased until they were reinstituted in 1859. These contests, like publications in periodicals, provided an economical entrée into the world of letters and therefore gave women writers a more accessible venue for circulating their work than was possible in the established publishing houses.

The first contest she won was for dramatic monologues. This genre was encouraged that year, and Albert was working on a piece called "La infanticida: Monòleg dramàtic en vers" ("The Infanticide: A Dramatic Monologue in Verse"), in which the speaker is a young woman. The organizers of the contest requested the presence of the author, with the expectation that the play would be performed. But Albert, a rural landowner from the agricultural and fishing village of L'Escala, on the Costa Brava, disliked publicity and did not attend, and the play was not staged. When it became known that the author of this harsh tale of rural life was a woman, scandal ensued, making her even more reluctant to appear in public. She discussed this bittersweet episode of triumph and rebuff in an interview given years later to Tomàs Garcés:

> I was given the award. There were fantastic arguments about who the author of the work was. Apparently, it was a bold, daring monologue. I didn't realize it. When they found out the author was a woman, the scandal was worse. They thought it unacceptable for me to write about an infanticide. But can the work of an artist have limits? I don't believe art can be restrained by moral norms. I believe it is fundamental to advocate for artistic freedom. Thanks to this independence, I have been faithful to my vocation, in which everyone has tried to intervene. (Català, "Conversa" 1748)[2]

Despite her success in publishing this and other early plays, she did not live to see "The Infanticide" performed; it was first staged in 1967. Partly as a result of the fuss surrounding the play, she began to use a masculine pseudonym, Víctor Català, and used it for the rest of her life.[3] The patriotic nom de plume taken by Albert was the name of the protagonist of a novel she never finished.

The other prize awarded to Albert in the 1898 contests at Olot was for the poem "El llibre nou" ("The New Book"), which expresses her love for books. Like many of her female contemporaries in Spain, she began her writing career by publishing poetry in periodicals, more accessible than books to both writers and readers. Ultimately she turned to narrative, which became the main body of her production. Turn-of-the-century Barcelona saw a flourishing of the literary marketplace for works in Catalan, but journals remained the more feasible venue for stories and even novels by women.

Catalan was Albert's language and the means of communication of the cultural establishment in which Albert moved. Yet as a minority and often suppressed language throughout the history of the Spanish nation-state, Catalan suffered long periods of scant production in literature, especially during the seventeenth and eighteenth centuries. In the nineteenth century, however, the time of Romanticism in other Western European countries, the political and cultural activity of the middle classes led to a blossoming that would become known as the Renaixença ("Renaissance"), a cultural revival of Catalan language and literature (see Resina, "Catalan Renaixença"). In Catalonia, as well as in the other two minority areas of Spain, Galicia and the Basque Country, the movement called for a resurgence not only of the autochthonous languages but also of national pride. This Romantic nationalist spirit spurred many women to write about the close relation between the individual subject and the land and led to an incipient modern feminism.

The publication in 1833 of Carles Aribau's ode "A la pàtria" ("To the Fatherland") in Catalan paved the way for the canonical male poets Jacint Verdaguer and Joan Maragall. Encouraged by this new patriotic fervor, a number of women began to write in Catalan during the second half of the century. Typically, they had begun to write in Castilian but changed to their own language. Their work is characterized by evocations of Catalonia, expressions of religious sentiment, maternal and family sensibilities, and in some cases, social and political criticism. There is also a search for rootedness in women's literature, in which the authors seek, find, and celebrate their literary foremothers. Josefa Massanés (1811–87), an early leader of a group of women intellectuals in Barcelona, was praised by Carolina Coronado (1823–1911) and written about by Dolors Monserdà (1845–1919). Monserdà was in turn lauded by Carme Karr (1865–1943) and Maria Aurèlia Capmany (1918–91), whose clandestine Catalan lessons during Franco's regime extended this tradition to her pupil Montserrat Roig (1946–91).

In an effort to foster primary and secondary education for young women, Francesca Bonnemaison established a library and cultural center for women in 1909 in Barcelona. Albert corresponded with Monserdà, the most prolific of the group, during the early part of the century, mostly regarding literary prizes. (In a eulogy for Monserdà, she complained that Monserdà's work had been unjustly underrated.) In addition to her creative work in various genres, Monserdà wrote essays on feminism, two of which were published as books: *El feminisme a Catalunya* ("Feminism in Catalonia") in 1907 and *Estudi feminista* ("Feminist Study") in 1909. She was the first woman president of the Jocs Florals.

With the Spanish Civil War (1936–39) and the ensuing dictatorship of Francisco Franco (1939–75), feminist activities among Catalan women writers were curtailed. But Albert's prolific correspondence continued and includes letters to younger writers such as Roser Matheu and Aurora Bertrana, the latter of whom is deeply indebted to the writer from L'Escala. Indeed,

Albert's long life traces a series of major political upheavals in Spain, beginning with the Carlist Wars, which pitted regional monarchists against a centralizing and liberalizing state apparatus that included federalists (advocates of regional autonomies in the Spanish state) and, in the 1860s and 1870s, antimonarchists. Albert's father, a man who believed in Catalan autonomy, was intensely involved in these conflicts. The Carlist Wars ended after a short-lived republic in 1873 and the restoration of a constitutional monarchy in 1876. By the end of the nineteenth century most Spanish colonial possessions were lost in a war with the United States, a cultural and political event that led to soul-searching by many intellectuals and writers, including Catalans. Literary historians have designated writers from this period as belonging to the Generation of 1898.

In the early twentieth century, as the entire peninsula, along with the Balearics and the Canaries, began (belatedly in relation to other parts of Europe) to suffer the growing pains of industrialization, labor unrest became particularly intense in Catalonia, a region whose textile factories were models of rising capitalism. Conflict between workers and industrialists allied with political elites culminated in 1909 in the Setmana Trágica ("Tragic Week") in Barcelona, a clash that also had to do with the vestiges of Spanish colonialism in northern Africa, since many soldiers who died in colonial wars were Catalan workers conscripted by the Spanish army. These upheavals, including the rise of fascism, continued into the 1930s, and they directly affected the wealthy Albert family. During the Second Republic (1931–39), the family house in L'Escala was ransacked by anti-Fascist soldiers in search of weapons. None were found, apart from a few antiques, but especially disturbing for Albert was the loss of some of her personal and literary documents.

Albert has earned a place in the canon of Catalan literature, and many consider her the model narrator of the late nineteenth to mid-twentieth century. Since her earliest work took place in a rural setting, she was considered a rural writer, but this label does not do her justice: she was a versatile author whose cultural milieu comprised a number of literary movements, including modernism. According to Joan Ramon Resina, Catalan modernism has much to do with an "urbanization of literature" ("Modernism" 514). Although Albert's early settings are rural, Albert by no means celebrates the country life. In fact, she debunks the Romantic myth of the happy yeoman. It is customary for critics to compare her work with that of Raimon Casellas (1855–1910), whose modernist novel *Els sots feréstecs* (1901; "Wild Ravines," translated by Alan Yates as *Dark Vales*) sets the individual in conflict with a hostile environment, with the hostility coming from other people and from nature itself. There also are many interesting similarities with the work of Pardo Bazán (1851–1921), a Galician writer who was branded a rural naturalist despite her great range: both Pardo Bazán and Albert were feminists *avant la lettre*, both narrated the harsh conditions of rural areas, and both were self-taught and achieved a level of education far surpassing that of most of their female contemporaries. Also, while in both there is a strong dose of social realism, there are traces of urban modernism as well.

Albert's settings are not all on farms or in villages; one novel and a number of stories have an urban background. *Caires vius* (1907; "Rough Edges") contains "Carnestoltes" ("Carnival," included in this volume), which has a Carnival setting, and "Capvespre" ("Eventide"), which makes references to the cinema. In *Jubileu* (1951; "Jubilee") almost half the stories take place in Barcelona, and several make use of the technique, at once modern and ancient, of indirect dialogue. There are also tales within tales, framed stories. Several critics, among them Jordi Castellanos (*Intel·lectuals* and "*Solitud*") and Núria Nardi, study Albert as a modernist writer while recognizing in her work characteristics of realism and naturalism. The only movement Albert rejected was *noucentisme*, which she found too stylized, idealistic, and limiting. Begun and described by Eugeni d'Ors, *noucentisme*, a term analogous to the Italian *novecento*, has to do with twentieth-century sensibilities that highlight cultural differences. The movement insisted, as modernism did, on the work of art principally as an aesthetic construct. Like other writers of the early twentieth century, Albert often asserted her artistic freedom, at times reacting against criticism of her work, of its subject matter and its use of experimental techniques rather than styles in vogue at the time. In *Caires vius*, she uses a long prologue, which she calls "Pòrtic" ("Portico"), to explain her views on certain literary movements as well as on the nature of literature.[4] Years later, she returns to the theme in *Contrallums* ("Backlighting"), where she maintains that literary currents are like the waters of a river that someone dyes: "A pinch of Prussian blue, for example, will dye a great expanse with its virulence, but a greater quantity of modest earth tone will subtly alter the color with light tints" (Català, *Obres* 814; see also Capmany). Prussian blue may represent *noucentisme*, with its rigid limitations and its efforts to normalize Catalan grammar and spelling according to rules that Albert rejected.[5] That realism, with its naturalist tendencies, characterizes many of her stories but does not preclude a certain lyrical flare, attention to the beauty of the surroundings of her characters, and great appreciation of the female body.[6] All in all, in her writing as in her life, Albert was sui generis: she lived and wrote at a distance from the mainstream; she sympathized with the plight of women but was not a declared feminist; and, as a well-to-do landowner, she feared the excesses of extremists on the left. Her comments of a political nature involved only issues of artistic and linguistic freedom.

Albert's literary production was interrupted by two long silences. After seven books of various genres appeared between 1901 and 1907, Albert published nothing more until the 1920s, when four new works of narrative came out. Fourteen more years elapsed before the publication of *Retablo* ("Retable"), her only work in Castilian. Her memoirs and two more collections of stories followed in the 1940s and 1950s. Maria Aurèlia Capmany, a well-known Catalan writer and political figure, analyzed these silences in her epilogue to the 1972 edition of Albert's complete works. Capmany suggests a combination of editorial and literary pressures to explain the lapses in production. One might also suspect social and family duties related to her quasi-aristocratic position in L'Escala. In any case, silence is a virtual protagonist in some of the stories; several rapes are dramatically silenced, and both "Carnival" and "Ànimes mudes" ("Silent Souls") are haunted by unspoken words.

Formal schooling was limited for Albert. She had strong ideas about what she wanted to learn, and, since her family was well-to-do, she preferred to hire tutors for specific interests, especially art. She read avidly and tells of regular visits to her home by a bookseller, from whom she bought whatever she fancied. Along with her early efforts in theater and poetry, she produced drawings, paintings, and sculptures, but just as Rodoreda would do some years later, Albert abandoned the visual arts to concentrate on narrative.[7] Being the oldest of four children and having a sickly mother and elderly grandmother to care for, she had to administer the family business on the death of her father, when she was twenty years old. She lived in the family residence all her life but traveled in Europe, especially to France and Italy, and maintained an apartment in Barcelona, where she went to the theater, seldom missing season premieres. She never married but had several lifelong friends and participated in the family life of her siblings. She also corresponded with many contemporaries, exchanging letters over a long period with the poet Joan Maragall, the dramatist Angel Guimerà, the novelist Narcís Oller, and her editors, among others. Albert's nonfiction includes *Mosaic*, a book of impressions and memories, various speeches and articles, interviews, and prologues to the works of others as well as her own. A study of these prologues reveals that Albert was also a sophisticated literary critic and theorist. In *Caires vius*, she writes an eloquent statement in favor of artistic freedom and originality—breaking the mold, as it were, of the literary fashions of the day, such as *noucentisme*. In a 1926 interview with Tomàs Garcés, she describes her work as "unbridled eclecticism" (Català 1749).

Albert's best-known work is the widely translated novel *Solitud* (*Solitude: A Novel of Catalonia*), set in a small hermitage in the mountains near L'Escala. The young protagonist, Mila, marries and moves to her isolated new home but soon finds that her husband is no company or help. She survives for a time in this difficult environment with the aid and sympathy of an elderly shepherd, who lends great lyricism to the work.

Folklore emanates from his telling of *rondalles*, or traditional
tales. *Solitud* is an intensely psychological narrative, a symbolic
description of female desire that centers on the ascent to and
descent from a mountaintop. The conclusion is open-ended:
the reader is left wondering about Mila's future. The protagonist of *Solitud* is a good example of Albert's distancing herself
from literary fashion, for Mila is neither a fin de siècle femme
fatale nor modernism's fragile nymph; she endures by aban-
doning home and husband.

Albert's second (and last) novel came out fifteen years later:
Un film (3.000 metres) ("A Film [Three Thousand Meters]") is
an innovative work whose structure is based on another of her
passions, the movies.[8] Reading its six carefully crafted chap-
ters, one can imagine a series of related films that follow the
development of the protagonist, Nonat, from a proud young
orphan in search of his roots to the princely leader of a band
of Barcelona criminals. The seamy streets are in total contrast
with the idealized city of *noucentista* writers, just as Nonat's
gruesome companions contrast with the fastidiously elegant
and handsome young man. When the novel was published, in
1926, the reviewers panned it, because it was too experimental for prevailing taste and perhaps also because its urban setting disturbed those who expected more ruralism from Albert.
Belittling both the novel and the seventh art, film, one critic
exclaimed, "If *Un film* were a film, . . . it would have no interest
at all: the genre, especially offscreen, offers few aesthetic possi-
bilities" (qtd. in Capmany 1865).

This volume's collection of Albert's work begins with "The
Infanticide," one of the eight plays Albert wrote early in her
career. The story begins in medias res and maintains dramatic tension throughout. As the work advances, the audience

begins to realize that the sole voice comes from within an insane asylum. The young woman unfolds her tale in verse, which is written in hendecasyllables and punctuated with symbols, especially the sickle wielded by her violent father, of whom she is terrified.

The ten stories that follow are taken from five collections; one story appeared only in a periodical. Readers will find a great variety of narrative techniques: multiple voices, distancing, breathtaking descriptions of nature in contrast with grotesque social situations, voluptuous presentations of the female body (see Bartrina 109–96), short vignettes as well as works long and complex enough to be considered novellas and published as single volumes. The stories from late in her life continue to show a great range in theme, character, and setting. Albert's works are populated with everyone from sophisticated doctors to depraved outcasts, but most of her protagonists are female, and friendship and solidarity among women feature prominently in a number of stories. Plants and animals are important to plot as well as in imagery.

I included two very different stories from the collection *Drames rurals* ("Rural Dramas"). A fatalistic outlook in "L'empelt" ("The Graft") can be compared with the determinism characteristic of naturalism as two brothers face off: a responsible son, of good stock, against a fatally flawed "graft" from another, inferior breed. Nature plays its part, as stormy weather accentuates the somber, tense scene. "L'enveja" ("The Craving") uses plant imagery in a lyrical piece written in hendecasyllables. Repetition of descriptive lines adds to the poetry of this tale: the protagonist is a "country goddess" with a basket on her head that seems to be made of "strands of woven gold"; her husband is "a goodly fellow from solid earth."

These lines open and close the story, forming a circle and acting as couplets in a poem.

The collection *Ombrívoles* ("Somber Shades") contains a short, poignant story dealing with old age and the end of life, "Conformitat" ("Acceptance"). Following a rural tradition, an old widower, realizing that his family function has ended, silently communicates his wishes to his deceased wife. "Ànimes mudes" tells of star-crossed lovers on neighboring farms: a family feud generations old keeps them from exchanging anything more than long, meaningful glances. In *Caires vius*, "Carnestoltes" tells how merrymaking on the streets annoys the aging and crippled Marquise of Artigues, for it is uncouth and rude, not the elegant masked balls she remembers from her youth. The relationship between mistress and maid develops with lesbian overtones (see Bartrina 164–70) and leads to a crisis of faith among displays of mysticism and silent, personal prayer. "Giselda" is one of several stories of Albert's that venture into myth. Composed as a fairy tale and based on a Catalan song with the theme of female vengeance similar to the play and opera *Tosca*, it ends in a brutality worthy of the Grimm brothers.

"Secretet rosa" ("The Rose-Colored Secret") appeared in *La il·lustració catalana* ("Catalan Illustration") in 1910 and was not reprinted until the publication of the second edition of Albert's *Obres completes* ("Complete Works") in 1972. It is a stylized piece in which the visual element is paramount, more a vignette than a narrative. Its allusions to Van Beers are a reminder that Albert's youth was dedicated to painting and sculpture. "La pua de rampí" ("The Pitchfork Prong"), from *Contrallums*, is painterly despite the violent, climactic scene of attack. The landscape is described as the protagonist takes her daylong walk; she and the reader experience impressionistic visions of changing light, shadow, and color.

The last two stories of this volume are from a much later collection, appropriately titled *Vida mòlta* ("Much Life"). In the family relationship of "La jove: Tot pastant" ("Kneadings of a Daughter-in-Law"), the bonding among women in a rural village defends and protects them against the perils of the patriarchal order. The central image is the baking of bread. Beleta's kneading takes on great sensuality, and more than once the narrative voice compares the rising dough to a woman's breast. The kneading room becomes something of a "room of one's own" at the same time, since Beleta's presence in the dark space often goes unnoticed and Beleta overhears crucial conversations that allow her to shape the outcome. (In two short, poetic pieces written in 1903 and published later in *Mosaic*, Albert describes her private space in the household, "Ma cambra blanca" ["My White Chamber"] and "Mon niu" ["My Nest"], anticipating Virginia Woolf's 1929 *A Room of One's Own* on a personal if not political level.) Several voices overlap in this masterful tale: Beleta's thoughts and memories contrast with dialogues that reflect the family's values. The men's voices are gruff, the women's fearful and timid. Finally, "Pas de comèdia" ("Parts in a Play") addresses role reversal when an oppressed and battered woman discovers her strength.[9]

Albert's linguistic range is wide, from narrative voices using borrowed and invented words to dialogues among illiterate peasants. In some works, poems and popular songs lend a lyricism beyond the carefully crafted imagery and systems of symbols. Her technical influence on later authors has been mentioned by some critics, notably Carles Cortés, but this aspect of her work is in need of further study.

Albert was honored as president of the Jocs Florals in 1917 and was the first woman to be elected to the Reial Academia de Bones Lletres ("Royal Academy of Literature") of Barcelona, in 1923. Appreciation for her work, however, faded with the advent of new writers, new aesthetics, and new critics. That trend is being reversed now. Recent editions of her writing and three major collections of essays about her, edited by Enric Prat and Pep Vila, have resulted from symposia sponsored by the cultural department of the city of L'Escala. Several scholars have taken up Helena Alvarado's 1984 plea for a reinterpretation of Albert ("Víctor Català"), and there notably new collections by Núria Nardi and by Lluïsa Julià (see "Works and Editions of Caterina Albert" below); a publication of her letters by Irene Muñoz i Pairet in two volumes; and, most important, a monograph by Francesca Bartrina on the complete works of Albert, a study in Catalan that is most insightful. It is my hope that these works and new translations will encourage the continued reevaluation of Albert.

Notes

[1] For a discussion of the development of languages and literatures of the Iberian Peninsula that questions the notion of a national literature, see Dagenais.

[2] Translations are mine.

[3] Gabriel Ferrater said in 1967 that it was ridiculous to continue calling her Víctor Català (255). Marta Pessarrodona echoed that opinion in 2004 (9). (Albert was not alone in using a male pseudonym. One of her contemporaries in Barcelona, Palmira Ventós i Cullell, wrote all her work as Felip Palma.)

[4] My translations of "Pòrtic"("Portico") and "El carcanyol" ("The Windfall"), both from *Caires vius* and both in *Obres completes*, are available as a free download from the MLA bookstore.

⁵Pompeu Fabra is the key figure in the normalization of Catalan. Working for the Institut d'Estudis Catalans ("Institute of Catalan Studies"), he produced *Normes ortogràfiques* in 1913, *Diccionari ortogràfic* in 1917, and *Gramàtica catalana* in 1918.

⁶Bartrina's study in Catalan of Albert is among the best and most complete. See particularly her thoughts on "Amor entre dones" ("Love among Women"), where she suggests that Albert may have been a lesbian (164–70). This possibility has not been explored by critics or biographers. In her literary biography of Albert, Muñoz does not go into personal matters.

⁷Rodoreda was the first woman to receive the Premi de les Lletres Catalanes ("Prize for Catalan Literature") for her lifetime work as a writer. She did a number of paintings in her early years but then turned to literature. Like Albert, she loved films. The autodidactic character of their educations may account in part for their great originality of expression.

⁸I mentioned Rodoreda's love for the movies. Gertrude Stein was a fan as well; she compared her writing techniques with sequences in a film. For Rodoreda, see McNerney 4; for Stein, see Lewis and Lewis 204.

⁹One finds another parallel in the striking similarity between Emilia Pardo Bazán's "Feminista" and Albert's "Pas de comèdia."

Works Cited and Consulted

Alvarado i Esteve, Helena. *"Solitud" de Víctor Català*. Empúries, 1997.

———. "Víctor Català / Caterina Albert, o l'apassionament per l'escriptura." *La infanticida i altres textos*, by Caterina Albert, LaSal, 1984, pp. 7–35.

Barnstone, Willis. *The Poetics of Translation: History, Theory, Practice.* Yale UP, 1993.

Bartrina, Francesca. *Caterina Albert / Víctor Català: La voluptuositat de l'escriptura*. Eumo, 2001.

Bergman, Emilie, and Paul Julian Smith, editors. *¿Entiendes? Queer Readings, Hispanic Writings.* Duke UP, 1995.

Bieder, Maryellen. "Albert i Paradís, Caterina." *Double Minorities of Spain: A Bio-bibliographic Guide to Women Writers of the Catalan, Galician, and Basque Countries*, edited by Kathleen McNerney and

Introduction

Cristina Enríquez de Salamanca, Modern Language Association, 1994, pp. 31–35.

Boccaccio, Giovanni. *The Decameron.* Selected, translated, and edited by Mark Musa and Peter E. Bondanella, W. W. Norton, 1977.

Capmany, Maria Aurèlia. "Epíleg: Els silencis de Víctor Català." Català, *Obres*, pp. 1851–68.

Casacuberta, Margarida, and Lluís Rius. "Caterina Albert i Paradís en el Certamen Literari D'Olot." *Els jocs florals d'Olot, 1890–1921*, Batet, 1988, pp. 36–40.

Castellanos, Jordi. *Intel·lectuals, cultura i poder: Entre el modernisme i el noucentisme.* Magrana, 1998.

———. "*Solitud*, novel·la modernista." *Els marges*, vol. 25, May 1982, pp. 45–70.

Castro-Paniagua, Francisco. *English-Spanish Translation, through a Cross-Cultural Interpretation Approach.* UP of America, 2000.

Català, Víctor. "Conversa amb Víctor Català." Interview by Tomàs Garcés, *Revista de Catalunya*, vol. 3, no. 26, 1926, pp. 126–34. Català, *Obres*, pp. 1747–55.

———. *Obres completes.* 2nd ed., Selecta, 1972.

Charlon, Anne. *La condició de la dona en la narrativa femenina catalana, 1900–1983.* Edicions 62, 1990.

Cortés i Orts, Carles. "L'empremta de la narrativa de Caterina Albert en els primers relats de Mercè Rodoreda." Prat and Vila, *II Jornades*, pp. 203–32.

Dagenais, John. "Medieval Spanish Literature in the Twenty-First Century." Gies, pp. 39–57.

Dingwaney, Anuradha, and Carol Maier, editors. *Between Languages and Cultures: Translation and Cross-Cultural Texts.* U of Pittsburgh P, 1995.

d'Ors, Eugeni. *Glosari, 1906–1910.* Selecta, 1950.

Epps, Brad, editor. "Introduction: Barcelona and Modernity." *Catalan Review*, vol. 18, nos. 1–2, 2004, pp. 13–28. Special issue on Barcelona and modernity.

Felski, Rita. *The Gender of Modernity.* Harvard UP, 1995.

Ferrater, Gabriel. "Solitud." U of Barcelona, 1966–67. Typescript.

Gies, David, editor. *Cambridge History of Spanish Literature.* Cambridge UP, 2004.

xxvii

Introduction

Gilabert, Joan. "Català, Víctor." *Dictionary of the Literature of the Iberian Peninsula*, vol. 1, edited by Germán Bleiberg et al., Greenwood, 1993, pp. 355–57.

Good, Kate. "Domestic Disturbances: Breaking the Mold of Female Comportment in Caterina Albert i Paradís' 'Pas de comèdia.'" *Catalan Review: International Journal of Catalan Culture*, vol. 29, 2015, pp. 23–39.

Lefevre, André. *Translating Literature: Practice and Theory in a Comparative Literature Context*. Modern Language Association, 1992.

Lewis, R. W. B., and Nancy Lewis. *American Characters*. Yale UP, 1999.

Maragall, Joan. "Un libro fuerte e incompleto." *Obres completes*, by Maragall, vol. 2, Selecta, 1960, pp. 197–98.

McNerney, Kathleen, editor. *Voices and Visions: The Words and Works of Mercè Rodoreda*. Susquehanna UP, 1999.

Miracle, Josep. *Víctor Català*. Alcides, 1963.

Möller-Soler, Maria-Lourdes. "Caterina Albert o la 'solitud' d'una escriptora." *Letras femeninas*, vol. 9, 1983, pp. 11–21.

Monserdà, Dolors. *Estudi feminista, orientacions per la dona catalana*. 1909.

———. *El feminisme a Catalunya*. Francesc Puig, 1907.

Muñoz i Pairet, Irene. "L'art plàstic de Caterina Albert." *Revista de Catalunya*, vol. 287, 2014, pp. 185–212.

———. *Caterina Albert / Victor Català, 1869–1966*. Vitella, 2016.

———, editor. *Epistolari de Víctor Català*. CCG, 2005–09. 2 vols.

———. "Glossa de Caterina Albert / Víctor Català." *Serra d'or*, vol. 688, 2017, pp. 47, 287–50, 290.

———. "Joan Maragall i Víctor Català, des del seu epistolari, 1902–1911." *Haidé*, vol. 4, 2015, pp. 41–51.

Nardi, Núria. Introduction. *Contes: Víctor Català*, by Caterina Albert, Bruño, 1994, pp. 9–53.

Pardo Bazán, Emilia. "Feminist." *"Torn Lace" and Other Stories*, translated by María Cristina Urruela, Modern Language Association, 1996, pp. 118–25.

Pessarrodona, Marta, editor. *Caterina Albert: Cent anys de la publicació de Solitud*. CSIC–Generalitat de Catalunya, 2007.

———. *Caterina Albert: Un retrat*. Generalitat de Catalunya, 2004.

Porter, Josep. *Els dibuixos de Víctor Català*. 1955.

Prat, Enric, and Pep Vila, editors. *Actes de les primeres jornades d'estudi sobre la vida i l'obra de Caterina Albert i Paradís "Víctor Català."* L'Abadia, 1993.

———. *Actes de les terceres jornades d'estudi sobre la vida i obra de Caterina Albert (Víctor Català)*. L'Abadia, 2006.

———. *II Jornades d'estudi: Vida i obra de Caterina Albert i Paradís (Víctor Català), 1869–1966*. L'Abadia, 2002.

Pujol, Josep. "Plomes veïnes: Caterina Albert vs. Marguerite Yourcenar." *Lambda*, vol. 80, 2014, pp. 1–3.

Rabassa, Gregory. *If This Be Treason: Translation and Its Dyscontents*. New Directions, 2005.

Resina, Joan Ramon. "The Catalan Renaixença." Gies, pp. 470–78.

———. "Modernism in Catalonia." Gies, pp. 513–19.

Ribera Llopis, Juan M. *Projecció i recepció hispanes de Caterina Albert i Paradís, Víctor Català, i de la seva obra*. CCG, 2007.

Riquer, Martín de, et al. *Història de la literatura catalana*. 11 vols. Ariel, 1988.

Rotella, Pilar. "Naturalism, Regionalism, Feminism: The Rural Stories of Emilia Pardo Bazán and Caterina Albert i Paradís." *Excavatio*, vol. 15, nos. 3–4, 2001, pp. 134–47.

Sobré (Sobrer), Josep Miquel. "Albert i Paradís, Caterina." *Women Writers of Spain: An Annotated Bio-bibliographical Guide*, edited by Carolyn Galerstein and Kathleen McNerney, Greenwood, 1986, pp. 13–15.

Vilarós, Teresa M. "Caterina Albert i Paradís ('Víctor Català')." *Spanish Women Writers: A Bio-bibliographical Source Book*, edited by Linda Gould Levine et al., Greenwood, 1993, pp. 12–22.

Villas i Chalamanch, Montserrat. *La morfologia del lèxic de Solitud de Víctor Català*. L'Abadia, 1999.

Yates, Alan. "*Solitud* i els *Drames rurals*." *Serra d'or*, vol. 11, 1969, pp. 646–48.

THE WORKS AND EDITIONS OF
CATERINA ALBERT

Albert's *Obres completes* includes not only the texts listed below but also some of her correspondence, speeches, prologues, and articles as well as a long introductory study by Manuel de Montoliu, the 1926 interview with Tomàs Garcés, and the article-epilogue by Maria Aurèlia Capmany. A new, revised edition is to be hoped for. Some of the pieces in this volume have newer editions, which I consulted.

El cant dels mesos. 1901.

Caires vius. 1907.

"Cendres" i altres contes. Introduced and edited by Lluïsa Julià, Pirene, 1995.
 A collection of stories from several books.

Contes. Introduced and edited by Núria Nardi, Bruño, 1994.
 A collection of stories from several books.

Contes diversos. Introduced and edited by Núria Nardi, Laia, 1981.
 A collection of stories from several books.

Contrallums. 1930.

De foc i de sang. Edited by Blanca Llum Vidal, selection and postscript by Lluïsa Julià, Club, 2017.

Drames rurals. 1902.

Drames rurals [and] Caires vius. Introduced and edited by Núria Nardi, Barcanova, 1992.

Un film (3.000 metres). 1920. Club, 2015.

"La infanticida" i altres textos. Introduced and edited by Helena Alvarado. LaSal, 1984.

Jubileu: Novíssims contes inèdits. Edited by Josep Miracle, Selecta, 1951.

Mosaic. 1946. Introduced and edited by Lluïsa Julià, Edicions 62, 2000.

Ombrívols. 1904. 2nd. ed, 1948.

Quatre monòlegs. 1901.

Retablo. Ediciones Mediterráneas, 1944.

Solitud. 1905. Edited by Núria Nardi, Edicions 62, 1990.

Teatre inèdit: La infanticida, Verbagàlia, Les cartes, L'alcavota. Edited by Josep Miracle, F. Camps Calmet, 1967.

Vida mòlta. Selecta, 1987.

In English

Solitude: A Novel of Catalonia. 5th ed., translated and introduced by David Rosenthal, foreword by the author. Readers International, 1992.

NOTE ON THE TRANSLATION

Albert first came to my attention when I went to Spain as a graduate student to study the poetry of Ausias March, but it would be years before I could devote the time to her that her complexity requires and before I would have the chance to travel to L'Escala to work on translating some of her narratives. I have tried to make these wide-ranging stories sound normal in American English without losing their rich linguistic variety, powerful expression, attention to detail, and lyricism. While this strategy might be called domestication, I have strived to render the local flavor of her prose as well. Despite the great divide between rural and industrial Catalonia of a century ago and our urban, postmodern, globalized time and space, Albert's close look at human nature gives universality to these works, and that universality helps the translator. In her prologues and other essays, she shows herself to be a theorist, but one can almost hear a weariness in her voice as she says in the "Pòrtic" ("Portico") to *Caires vius*, "[W]e prefer to work than to theorize, even though the work might turn out defective while the theory seems perfect, for too much theory creates traps and hindrances to the free impulse of action" (Català

597). Although she is referring to literature, I would apply her words to translation as well.

Two of the stories in this volume were written in hendecasyllables, and the dramatic monologue in them uses line separations. I tried to stay within those parameters as much as possible to retain the poetic rhythm. But for "L'enveja" I chose clarity instead of trying to capture the poetry. "La pua de rampí" presented special problems, beginning with the title itself. A *rampí* is a specialized rake, but for English speakers it conjures up an instrument that is incapable of its role in the story; a pitchfork serves better and is familiar to all. The use of proper names or those indicating profession or place in a family structure created difficulties—for example, the tendency in rural Catalonia to call people by their relation to one another instead of by a given name would be confusing and awkward in English. A story might never name its protagonist, referring to her instead as Pubilla. Literally the word means "heiress," but *heiress* has connotations in English that misrepresent the rural reality: the young woman stands to inherit the family farm, but she is not wealthy. Instead of baptizing her Maria, Núria, or with some other name, I ended up using Pubilla as her first name. Although Beleta of "La jove: Tot pastant" has a name, she is often called simply "la jove." Literally this term means "the young one," but here it specifically means "daughter-in-law." Her in-laws do not have names; they are called "el sogre," "la sogra," and "la cunyada," but so much repetition of "in-law" would be awkward in English, so I alternated between those forms and "the old lady," "the old man," and "the youngest sister." In "L'empelt," the characters are called "l'avi," "el noi," and "el petit" ("the grandpa," "the kid," and "the little one"), even though all are adults. While the first two terms can work in English, "little one" had to be changed to "younger brother" or sometimes, when he was intruding, "the intruder."

Finally, two stories were challenging because of their special style. "Giselda" is recounted as a fairy tale, using formulaic, stylized, repetitive language that had to be rendered into English in a similar vein. The extreme stylization of "Secretet rosa" enhances the visual effect and painterly quality of the tale. Dialogues, always tricky, must sound natural, and it is my hope that the Catalan peasants in translation don't sound too much like a professor of Spanish literature from West Virginia University.

Work Cited

Català, Victor. *Obres completes*. 2nd ed., Selecta, 1972.

CATERINA ALBERT

"Silent Souls"
and Other Stories

THE INFANTICIDE
A Dramatic Monologue in Verse

Sole character: NELA

The sparse cell of an insane asylum; at the back, a door with iron bars, which opens onto a whitewashed corridor. In the right corner, a bed; scattered about are the usual and necessary objects found in such places. Seated on the bed, NELA is huddled over with her head in her hands, her fingers curled into unruly hair. She wears a nightshirt of plain cloth with an open neckline; it is discolored, wrinkled around the neck, and has sleeves to the elbow, similar to those worn by peasants fifty years earlier. The skirt part is old, frayed by bleaching, the waist piece a dark yellow satin, a kind of sash that can also serve as a scarf around the neck. She's barefoot. She is young, pale, with the wild look of the insane. In the arrangement of the stage as well as in the character, the most absolute realism must prevail. If necessary for a greater effect, a few people can go back and forth

---

The Infanticide premiered the evening of 14 March 1967, starring Àngels Molls, at the Palau de la Música Catalana, in Barcelona.

beyond the bars — employees of the asylum, visitors, and so on; they may even pause for a moment to look silently at the scene. NELA remains in the position described for a few moments after the curtain rises; then she gets up, disturbed, rubbing her eyes, and she slowly moves toward the foreground, peering resentfully at the audience. She moves around freely, getting up, sitting down, pacing, so that the monologue will remain lively.

Keep in mind that NELA is not wicked but a young woman blinded by passion; she acts not of her own will but forced by circumstances, with her spirit imprisoned by two inflexible parallels: her love for Reiner and fear of her father; the first pulling her toward guilt, the second providing punishment. Together, they lead her to madness.

What are all these people doing here? . . . What I
   thought was . . .
It's always the same! . . . They told me
once I was inside this place
no one would see me again . . . It was a lie . . .
Everyone has lied to me, everyone, on purpose;
Don Jaume first, the owner's son.
Here too, just as up there, they stare
and they keep asking me, always following me around . . .
They even laugh . . . Damn them! . . . Oh, if
   I could just

                        (Making fists in rage.)

get out of here and by moonlight
run away through the fields, to the farm . . .

(Suddenly terrified.)

To the farm? . . . Oh, no, no! . . . Father is there,
he'll keep chasing me to cut my throat . . . One day

(In a low voice, full of dread.)

he showed me that twisted sickle,
shinier than a silver mirror,
sharper than a harvest knife . . .
He grabbed me by the arm with iron fingers,
and, waving it in my face,
"Take a good look," he said. "I'm keeping it
to cut off that witch head of yours
the day you defy me or dishonor me . . .
Take a real good look, whorehouse bitch, and
    remember
that I'm still strong enough, and this is not dull!" . . .
And watching me aslant, as he'd been doing
for a while, he shoved me down
and went off to the grindstone and . . . ground it more . . .

(Imitating the sound of grinding, horrified.)

Every *shist!* . . . *shist!* . . . went through my soul,
melting the marrow of my bones . . .

(Terrified, lowering her voice.)

But . . . he was too late . . . Days had gone by
since the special one started coming through the hayloft,

5

and we'd been seeing each other at the gorge
  and the ravine
while father and my brothers slept peacefully . . .

                         (Short pause; then, agitated.)

As soon as they finished the rosary
I served them dinner right away;
and since they were worn out from working
the grindstone or the hoe since dawn,
they went to bed as soon as the last bite was gone
and slept like newborn babes . . .
As soon as I heard their snores, I went
barefoot, groping through the cellar,
crossing the pony corral,
I'd turn through the fullery and the arcade,
already found by the hunting dog,
who followed me around like a lamb,
I got to the orchard and breathed, happily . . .
Often, the light of the stars dazzled me
with its twinkling, and the sky seemed
a field sown with bits of glass . . .

                              (Disheartened.)

The freshness and quiet air were so sweet! . . .
I could have stayed a good while there,
beneath the grapevine or the pomegranate! . . .
but he was waiting nearby, with open arms
and a kiss, or a hundred, or a thousand on his lips,

ready to cover my face with them
the moment I arrived . . . I was anxious,
trembling for fear of not finding him . . .
And barefoot, rushing like a startled animal
over the grass damp with dew,
I grabbed a jasmine, a rose,
to take to my Reiner . . . What anguish,
if when I gave a blackbird's whistle
I didn't hear from beyond the gully
another blackbird, full of joy!
Not running now, I flew eagerly,
as if life were pulling me there . . .
And . . . before I knew it I felt myself imprisoned
in arms like iron, but trembling too,
with a thousand kisses covering my neck and lips
and I was smothered in his breath; it burned me up
and I gave in, like a prodded sheep . . .

(Brief pause.)

I returned to this world . . . I don't know the hour . . .
when God wished or when . . . he wished . . .
because I wasn't myself . . . I did what he wanted,
I wasn't in control . . . since I loved him
more than anything in the world! . . . Before I saw him
I was like a savage beast.
I spat at everyone, kicking,
I lived among piglets, in stables,

I didn't even speak well . . . My father
didn't pay much attention to his girl;
he had other work with mills and lands!
and he, the special one . . . taught me everything . . .
    First, manners,
then, to be neat and tidy . . .
so that, in two months' time, he changed me so,
and the neighbors didn't even recognize me.
I still don't know how to thank him!
It seemed as if God was whispering in my ear,
telling me everything I should do . . .

                                        (Brief pause.)

From beginning to end, my whole life
became a desire, a moonlit night,
for it was only possible to see him at night . . .
I couldn't leave him! . . . It always seemed that
if I left him, I'd lose him forever . . .
a whole day without him seemed endless . . .
Twenty-four hours without kisses! . . .
twenty-four hours without feeling his cheek
snuggling between my breasts so sweet,
and his eyelids pressing against my lips! . . .
And they wanted me to leave him forever!
One day someone told my father
that I was seeing someone, a higher-up . . .

Some gossip who'd never known love . . . a dried-up
    soul, a cold log who now
should be burning in hell for what he did . . .
Because of the harm that was done! . . . From that day on
my father acted crazy, always watching me
like an evil spirit, forever snarling at me.
While he treated the mule and the blind cow
like daughters, spoiling them,
I was more a sow, or mule, for him.
Why? All because of my love's higher station! . . .
That's what caused Father's rage! . . .
As if being a gentleman were the greatest of sins,
the kind of cursed people
one should flee like the devil . . .
My Reiner must have been
a real devil for my father . . .
But I never knew why he feared him so! . . .
for he was so much nicer than the others,
he was bold, so brave they all envied him,
and a better hunter than my oldest brother,
and danced more gracefully than any young man
within five or six hours from here . . .
For I watched him well enough that evening
when the Baroness had a great feast
with all those people from Barcelona

9

who came to spend the summer in the village . . .
He knew all the dances . . . I watched him ever so well
from outside . . . with such a fine group.
I could neither breathe nor leave! . . .
The next day, he told me;
the dancing was his duty, but he was bored with it
and missed being at the gully, with his poor Nela . . .
But I could have sworn, while he danced,
he enjoyed it . . . I was so innocent!

(Pause.)

And besides, wasn't he handsome? . . . more than the vicar,
who everyone in the village
said looked just like Jesus . . . And a good man too? . . .
My Lord, he was! . . . I knew it well enough,
many times I felt tempted
to kneel down before him
and slowly say Our Father
like in front of the Christ statue at chapel! . . .
He seemed . . . what can I say? . . . a very different kind
    of man,
I don't know . . . so delicate . . .
he made you want to be near him . . .
With his eyes, he drew in your head and heart
as if you drank too fast . . .
People did what he wanted

even before he asked . . . and he thanked them

with hugs and kisses and great gestures

worth more than land and vines,

for everyone died of joy and then came back . . .

If he came late and I said so,

he stopped my complaint at my lips

(and he prayed litanies into my ear)

in who knows what language . . .

the sweetest, for sure, of all those spoken . . .

A language peasants don't know,

for at the mill I never heard it,

though my father says all the best landholders

of the region gather there.

(Mockingly.)

All the best landholders! . . . Don't make me laugh! . . .

All the finest heirs . . . Country bumpkins

with a pittance, a carnation behind their ears,

with their smelly drinks always at their lips,

their messed-up, faded shirts,

hairy arms . . . They're gallant, all right! . . .

They made me feel like fainting . . . If they came near,

it was to curse and say ugly things:

"Will you come to dance at the farmyard Sunday,

with us, outside, or to play cards?"

And they yakked about nothing, showing off,

staring at me from top to bottom, as if they
  owned me,
puffed with vanity, their eyes half-closed,
just like Lady Restituta,
the languid Lady Baroness . . .
And to court me, what did they do? . . .
They pinched and squeezed me so
that many times I thought I would faint . . .

(Angry and disgusted.)

Those guys pleased my father!
More than one tried to be his son-in-law . . .
But me?! . . . God keep me from those men,
smelling of dog from their fermenting sweat,
after seeing the other one, clean as a lily,
with fragrances of jasmine and honeysuckle,
and a thousand other unknown perfumes
of the rich, from the city, a good family . . .
He was so lovely! . . . Who could offer me
the pleasure I found at his chest,
feeling all reason fading away, little by little
as I drowned sweetly, as if inside
a garden bursting with moonlight! . . .

(Sweetly, ecstatically.)

Oh, Reiner, my Reiner! . . . My key to life,
why don't you come to see me? . . . I miss you so . . .
I'm so lonely, Reiner . . . all alone,

all day and all night in this room
waiting for your arms to hold me

                (She embraces herself tightly.)

like this, against your heart, like before . . .

                    (Her arms fall sadly.)

See? . . . This isn't it . . . I can't do it . . .

                (Pinching her arms with rage.)

They're like arms of dust, my poor arms! . . .
They offer neither joy nor torture.
They don't make me lose my breath, or scare me, like
    yours! . . .

               (Growing more and more excited,
              as if speaking to someone she can see.)

Reiner! Oh, my Reiner! . . . I want you to come,
right away, now, I want to see you! . . .
Can't you hear me, Reiner? . . . I don't even feel like
    eating,
I only want your kisses, always! . . .
I'm keeping them inside, between my lips,
millions of kisses, to give them to you all the time,
for years and years, until the end of the world . . .
I can't keep them anymore . . . they want to run
through the whole world till they find you,
but I don't even want my kisses to get there
before I do . . . I'm jealous
and love you above all things, forever and ever! . . .

You're coming to get me, yes?

As soon as your work is finished? . . . If you only knew

the things that have happened since you left!

Remember the night you left? . . . that night

we said good-bye in the straw loft? . . .

You held me in your arms and swore,

consoling me with kisses, as you drank the water

from the fountain of my eyes,

that you only had two or three months left

to finish your studies . . . and once they were done,

you'd come to the village like lightning,

fast as you could, to get me? . . .

Remember, Reiner, I embraced you then,

and holding you tight, slowly, I don't know if you

   heard me,

I whispered: "Ah, Reiner my love! . . . I think . . . I think

that something . . . something is happening,"

and you looked at me, like so, all delighted, so that

I laughed, even though I didn't feel like laughing.

How terrible! You didn't understand me at first,

then you did. What does it matter? . . . Don't you

remember what I mean? . . .

                        (Suddenly fearful.)

Well, it was true! . . . too true! . . .

Such heartbreak since that day! So much suffering! . . .

If anyone even looked at me, I turned red,

I felt burning coals in my cheeks . . .
I was terrified that everyone could see
everything, just by looking at me . . .

(*Brief pause.*)

One day, my father
stared at me up and down . . . "Why don't you eat? . . .
All you do is spit." "Because a fly fell into my plate." . . .
   A lie,
but I stiffened up completely
when he looked at me like that, and that question . . .
Even more . . . when I watched him stand up
and get the sickle off the hook . . . and he looked
   at it . . .
Oh, good God, what terror! . . . I could almost feel
the *zast!* right here . . .

(*Miming the cutting of her throat, horrified.*)

He did promise to do it,
and he's a man who keeps his word,
and his temper, I know it well . . . He'd have killed me
if he found out . . . and if I'm not mistaken,
he half-suspected it that night . . .
And me, what was I going to do
to keep it from showing? . . . It was impossible! . . .
Time was passing! . . . As if on purpose,
all the times I waited for you, the days
were long, so very long, they consumed me,

never ending! . . . Later, when I would have wanted

each day to last five years,

they rushed by in the blink of an eye . . .

The time was coming, so quickly . . .

How was I going to do it, all alone,

unprotected, without you or mother,

always seeing THAT, shining in the dark,

behind the door, that twisted sickle

waiting to cut my throat? . . .

My God, that sickle! Such dread!

No matter how hard I tried, even with my eyes closed

I could see it sparkle here, inside . . .

> (*Touching her forehead, she goes on*
> *with terror, in a low voice.*)

I can see it now! Even when I'm asleep! . . .

> (*Pause.*)

One day I heard Ciset, the helper,

talking to Tana

when she came to grind wheat . . . She was saying:

"Haven't you noticed, Ciset, the girl

has got so fat, in such a short time?"

And when he heard that, he laughed,

like a wolf, and he scared me.

"What are you laughing about?" she asked.

"Nothing, Tana, nothing at all . . . We'll soon be seeing

some big goings-on here, they'll be writing ballads . . .

As for me, at the end of the month, I'll ask for my pay
and these parts won't be seeing me anymore.
I don't like having anything to do with the
    authorities."...
She didn't quite understand what he meant,
but I did . . . the conversation stabbed me
right in the heart, like a needle . . .
So Ciset knew . . . what shame!
My father would realize it too, soon enough,
and my brothers, the neighbors, the whole village . . .
What gossip must be rumbling around, at the tavern!

(Brief pause; ashamed.)

And in the meantime, Reiner, you didn't come,
and more than seven months had gone by . . .
I wanted to let you know what was going on,
but, poor me! I don't know how to write,
and to have someone else write it, impossible! . . .
If you had been close by, it would've been different;
I'd have gotten the courage right away;
but all alone, I was going mad.
I had strong urges to do something crazy . . .
Throw myself into the pond, or from the roof,
hang myself with a cord . . . But how dreadful!
There were people at the mill all the time,
lots of people . . . grinding wheat
at all hours; it was a good year . . .

And I was dying of anxiety . . . Carrying the biggest sacks
from the line on my shoulders . . .
my legs failed me . . .

(Full of rage.)

I was up there all the time!
to see if the devil would take me . . .
If only he would, just like that!
It was no good pulling in on that sash
until blood came out of my mouth,
no good to beat myself
as my father did the mule . . . my time was here!
I couldn't stop it! Everyone would know,
and the sickle, in an instant . . .

(Terrified.)

would do its job! . . .

(Short pause; then, with growing dread.)

Finally, the time came . . . one evening . . .
the mill couldn't take on any more work,
it already had enough for two weeks . . .
My father, the help, and my brothers were
exhausted; they were asleep on their feet,
had all been working the last three nights . . .
And the mill had to keep going,
we had to keep the neighbors happy
no matter what . . . My father
swore, at dinner: "Damn it all!

I've asked several of them to help
so we can get caught up, I begged them,
I offered them a share; and they all say
we can't, we're all done in; it's impossible.". . .
"I'm exhausted," murmured the younger;
and Ciset and the older too: "We're even worse off!"
That's when I, all trembling and scared,
say to my father, without looking him in the eye:
"I can do it, if you like, I'll do the job." . . .
My father turns his head. "You, all by yourself?"
"I have the strength . . . I'm better than nothing."
"Well, all right, if you like . . . but . . . ," he says,
already tempted to rest a little.
I jumped up and lit the lamps, and was ready!
Here, here! . . . everyone to bed! . . . "Around two
come and get me . . . I won't sleep the whole night,"
replies my father, and I: "Go on, then, go!" . . .
Off they all go . . . Ah, I had to!
I'd been biting my lips for a while already
to keep from letting out the screams
that were coming up my throat, choking me . . . What
    torture!
So I went to the mill . . . just about dragging myself . . .
    and there . . .

> *(With horror, speaking slowly,*
> *as if seeing dreadful things.)*

That's where . . . it happened . . . the rolling of the
  millstones
muffled the cries . . . And how I suffered!
I suffered so, Reiner, all alone! . . .
Alone, no . . . then . . . when she was born . . .
She was tiny, like a doll . . .
with the most darling little face!
Eyes closed, mouth open . . .
I loved her right away!
She'd made me suffer so, but it didn't matter,
not at all, poor little thing!
It seemed I'd had her for years,
that I'd have her forever . . . Yes, forever! . . .

> *(All this with great tenderness, gratified by the memory;*
> *from here to the end, with anxiety, terror, delirium*
> *increasing as the words and situation warrant.)*

Poor, darling baby! . . .

> *(Suddenly listening, full of dread.)*

Can you hear the mill?! Turning, rolling, like . . . that
  day . . .

> *(She runs from one side to the other, frantic.)*

O Holy Virgin of Succor . . . Stop
that turning, rolling, or make me deaf! . . .
My brain is jumping and jumping,
I can hear the noise from here, inside . . .

> *(Pause. Then she spins quickly, as if answering someone.)*

How did it happen? . . .

(Full of pain.)

Oh, no! Don't make me say it! . . .

I'm cold . . . and afraid . . . I . . . I . . . that's not what I
    wanted . . .

I don't know how it happened . . . I was so happy,

when I saw the baby girl, I hugged her

and kissed her . . . I'd have smothered her with kisses,

I couldn't kiss her enough . . .

and I squeezed her so much, that the baby,

you see, she wrinkled up her face

and started to cry . . . a real shriek! . . . I turned

to stone, just like Saint Just's statue . . .

And the baby, what screams! . . . She seemed crazed . . .

I was so scared, I lost all reason . . .

then heard it . . . what terror! . . . Someone was coming,

I heard barefoot steps . . .

It was my father, for sure! . . . Virgin Mary!

What on earth was I going to do, I'll be damned!

They were quick steps . . . up the stairs . . .

And . . . I don't know . . . what happened . . . I saw the
    sickle

shining, all of a sudden . . . here, inside . . .

(Pointing to her head.)

I jumped up . . . the baby . . . again . . .

I cover her mouth . . . but . . . she won't stop crying . . .

21

and my father . . . he's close . . . I . . .

run to the . . . the mill . . . and . . . dear God! . . .

> *(With the deepest horror, squatting down and*
> *imitating the action of throwing something.)*

What a noise she made! . . . Completely squashed! . . .

And still she let out a howl! . . . A screech! . . . Let me

go! . . .

> *(She turns violently one way and the other,*
> *as if to free herself from someone.)*

I don't want to say anything else! . . . Stop the mill,

the devil is turning it . . . to kill me . . .

Father . . . it wasn't my father . . . I don't know who it

was . . .

who came in . . . inside there . . . I don't remember . . .

Lots of people . . . lots . . . Everyone stared at me,

with eyes wide! . . . like owls . . .

But my father . . . knows nothing . . . Don't let it out . . .

Everyone be quiet . . . shut up, everyone . . . because if

he knew,

with one sickle blow . . . my head would be on the

ground.

> *(Begging, with vivid anxiety.)*

Don't tell him, for the love of God, don't tell my

father! . . .

Nothing about the baby, not a peep . . . don't let him

suspect . . .

that's why I left my home
and I'm in here . . . so he won't find me . . .
That's what Don Jaume said . . . the owner's son . . .
Until Reiner comes . . . and we go to France . . .

> *(She curls up in a corner, and her*
> *voice gets lower gradually.)*

far away from father . . . and the sickle . . . and that . . .
mill . . .
I don't want . . . any other . . . baby girl . . .
to get crushed . . . ever again . . .

> *(At the end, she is barely audible. She says the last lines*
> *with a lost look, as if in a trance. The curtain descends on*
> *the next to last line, stops a meter and a half above the*
> *stage, and then, at the last word, falls suddenly.)*

THE GRAFT

"Hi, Kid, you've done me a few favors, and I'd like to return them, maybe saving you from a fit of rage."

"What's up, Pau?"

"Keep an eye on your patio: I think somebody's courting your chickens."

"Whoa! You think they'd dare, right in my own house?"

"A few days ago I saw a man standing next to the little patio door: when he saw my light, he flew the coop and I couldn't recognize him. But yesterday, when I finished the first patrol around town, he was standing there in the same place . . . I didn't like the looks of that, so I thought I'd let you know. So, now you know, and it's up to you: I've done my duty."

"I thank you for it, Pau, but come on . . . Everybody knows that I can send out some pretty good buckshot from the little opening in my room at anyone who dares to get into the house, and I doubt if there are too many who'd put themselves in the line of fire . . ."

The Kid smiled with the confidence of a good hunter whose nerve has never failed.

"One way or another, be forewarned, believe me, I have some experience and I can tell you I didn't like the way it looked."

"Don't worry, Pau, and thanks a lot for the warning."

"You're welcome, that's my job."

They said good-bye and went their separate ways.

Pau, the town watchman, swung his good jacket over his shoulder and went down the hill to get the best price he could for some corn he needed to fatten the calves. Kid Ordis, with his staff tucked under his arm, started to poke around the market, stopping at some of the stands, checking out the pairs of poultry offered by peasant women, sticking his hand into his neighbor's sack of bird feed to check the yield from that harsh field, pausing to exchange a few words with an out-of-towner he knew.

Suddenly feeling an arm on his shoulder, he turned his head: his brow wrinkled immediately with a look of disgust that involuntarily overtook him whenever he saw his brother.

The watchman looked at the two men from a dozen paces away, and he couldn't help saying to the corn seller:

"I'll be damned! Who could tell those two are blood brothers? The Kid and the younger Ordis . . . One as good as gold, and the other a son of a bitch . . . if God doesn't do something about him soon, he'll end up in jail."

"You're right . . . Old Man Ordis was great at grafting, but he sure blew that one! He had excellent stock, and he stuck that rotten branch onto it . . ."

The corn vendor, pleased with his comparison, let out a great laugh, showing all his big, yellow teeth and wine-colored gums, like a neighing horse.

"Well, if the penitents had to go to Rome, the old man would have had to join them. I heard him say, more than once, with his head hanging down: 'To think that I did such a thing of my own free will . . . !' And he meant the youngster, you know?"

"Yeah, of course!"

It was true. Old Ordis was a widower at forty, with a twelve-year-old son, and without even knowing why — whether out of a widower's boredom, or just the pull of the blood, which always ends up badly, as he would say remorsefully — he'd gotten involved secretly with the worst woman in town, kind of old, ugly, dirty, with a past as dark and wrinkled as a shroud, who was so fond of booze that she could pass out standing up anywhere in the middle of the afternoon. The end of a line of scoundrels, no one had ever approached her for any good reason. Ordis was a sensible man, a hard worker, well thought of and with prospects, and he wanted to do what many others had done: but suddenly . . . the most inconceivable thing happened. He consulted his conscience—for he was a man who had one—and, recognizing that there was no doubt and that it was God's punishment for lack of respect for his dead wife, he married the old boozer to give a name to that extra son sent to him as punishment for his sins.

No one could believe it, no one could get over such a strange marriage, considering who the two people were. That Ordis's scruples would lead to that! But in spite of it all, ashamed and convinced that the rest of his life would be misery, he went ahead with the plan. He never had a happy face again; from that moment on, no one saw him without a look of worry and sorrow.

The woman turned out to be as useless as she was foolish; she was the scandal of the neighborhood. Their son was a dissolute rascal: at six, he was caught stealing from the cash register at a store; at thirteen, he was sent up for a knife fight in a bar. When his father tried to bawl him out, he'd look the old man straight in the eye with the most insulting, tranquil stare, completely insensitive to words or slaps. When the old man saw that, he'd go to his room, trembling with anger and shame, and cry, pulling his hair and blaming himself for everything that had happened.

He died with that cross to bear after giving all his love to his older son—a good worker, excellent person, serious, intelligent—asking the Kid with all the humility of a sinner to have mercy on his little brother, who wasn't to blame for the dishonor that had befallen their household.

With the old man dead, the headaches passed on to the Kid, who had all kinds of problems with his brother. He soon threw him out of the house for causing every sort of trouble there, including beating mercilessly on his simple-minded mother. So the Kid found himself in court, with his little brother asking for his share of the inheritance. The youngster was officially an adult, so his older brother paid in full, and from then on they hardly looked at each other. But the older—everyone still called him the Kid—was sick at heart and filled with shame every time the Little One caused talk in the town with one of his feats. That's why the Kid couldn't even hear him mentioned without his heart skipping a few beats and that wrinkle showing up on his face, full of alarm and disgust.

So when he felt that hand on his shoulder at market, he took a step backward with that inevitable gesture of repulsion.

"Hey, Kid," he said with his annoying laugh.

"Hello," he responded drily. "What do you want?" For he knew that when his brother approached him, it was to get something out of him. Nor did the younger brother hide it.

"My wife has to make bread, and there's no wood for the oven. Could you let me have an armful?"

"Go to the house and help yourself."

Without waiting to be thanked, the Kid turned around and walked away, but he'd be a grouch for the rest of the day. He didn't stop at any more stands at the market or talk to anyone. To dispel the bad humor he left town and then took another walk in the afternoon.

At dusk he went home, and his wife said:

"That damn brother of yours came by and spent half an hour at the top of the woodpile, taking the best logs and telling me you said it was okay . . . I wanted to stop him, but he scares me, with that feline face always about to attack."

A bonfire of anger lit up his blood, but to avoid useless arguments, he just asked for a lantern and went out to check the outside doors.

He examined the whole house routinely, looking here and there distractedly. Since everyone knew he slept with the rifle at his headboard and he was an excellent shot, he wasn't at all afraid of the townspeople, but it was always possible a no-good stranger could pass through town.

After he'd looked the house over, he went out to the patio to check the little door that opened to a deserted part of the street, far from the bedroom window. It was the door Pau was talking about, the only place that might be a little vulnerable, but everything was normal.

He went into the patio shed: they used the top part as a granary and the lower part for the birds and some straw. The chickens, awakened from their transversal perches, bristled when they saw the light and came down with their necks sticking out, clucking, their round eyes glazed before the lamp. The immobile flame lightened the shadows around the Kid, and in the darkness the bright crests looked like blobs of blood.

Passing through them to get the ladder to the granary, Kid Ordis said to himself, looking at those sleepy birds:

"We'll see what smart ass tries to touch them! He'll leave his skin behind!"

At the very top there was a space with only two openings: the little horizontal door to the stairs and a window opening to the patio above the woodpile. Two esparto ropes held a bar like a trapeze, and the sacks were hanging from the bar, to keep them safe from rats. There were piles of oats, barley, and wheat on the floor, and lined up against the wall were strings of straw baskets, their cylindrical bellies holding chicken feed, dark as mulattas, flat beans and vetch, fair as a maiden's skin . . . the fruit of the entire harvest, not yet prepared for market.

The owner, with the handle of the lantern hanging from his fingers, stopped at each pile and examined everything carefully, pleased with the light-yellow barley, looking just like a smooth pool of refined oil, concerned about the bits of weed peeking up here and there in the oats, sticking his hand nervously into the wheat, to see if it was warm . . .

He got to the window and raised the lantern: one of the bolts was loose, and he started to tighten it, but when he touched it, the bolt came off in his hands, as if it were only held there by saliva. He looked at it, surprised, and realized he was holding the key as well. He pulled on the other bolt; it was loose too and would come right out. His heart jumped, and, setting the lamp down, he examined the entire window carefully. All the hardware on the other side of the wood had been undone, and with a slight push would come right out. He went pale: the thieves weren't after his chickens, as Pau assumed, but after his whole crop! Good thing he'd been forewarned!

He left the light on in the granary and went to the house to fetch a blanket and his shotgun, ready to spend the night on watch. He grabbed a bite of dinner, telling his wife only about what Pau had said and that he wanted to fire a couple of shots in the air to discourage anyone from coming near: he didn't explain the rest for fear of scaring her.

Back at the granary, he spread the blanket out on the ground and sat down, covering the lamp with a corner of it, and, with his weapon at hand, he waited.

It was a thick, overcast night; the moon was out, but wide bands of dark clouds, moving lazily across the sky, kept covering it up. The heavy air suggested an approaching storm, and every once in a while gusts of strong wind made the fig branches from the neighboring patio brush against the wall of the shed with a sharp sound, like scraping fingernails. From time to time, a rooster's nervous, penetrating cry, like a warning signal, pierced into the space.

The Kid was used to going to bed early and he got sleepy right away. To keep awake, he uncovered the light and started to listen to all the sounds coming from outside. Luckily, groups of young revelers passed by, making lots of noise all the way down the street to catch the attention of young women already retired in their homes. Their laughing shouts kept him alert, and his oil lamp as well, which flickered and glowed as if it wanted to join the fun. But as it got late, the noises faded away and all that was left was the scratching of the fig branches and the hours ringing from the bell tower, falling heavily like drops and resounding calmly, suspended, vibrating in the air before reaching the ground. The lamp contracted too and became still at the wick, as if ready to take a little nap, and the Kid, tilting his head to one side, drifted off a couple of times without even realizing it. His head drooping a bit too far was what woke him up, startled and alarmed, as if he were caught failing at his job. He'd rub his eyes, move his shoulders, shake his head or scratch his ears, and that would keep him awake for a while before he fell back into a light sleep. He didn't want to smoke, for it would signal an alarm, and he didn't know what to do to keep from drifting off. Meantime, the sounding of the hours seemed to slow down, falling lazily and monotonously from the tower: the long ones had already finished and the short ones were beginning when a certain scratching noise that didn't sound like a fig tree awakened the watchman with a start. He instinctively placed one hand on the shotgun and with the other covered the lamp. It went out quickly, and all was completely dark.

The sound was coming from the woodpile: someone was stepping carefully over the logs, making them moan with short, dry squeaks.

The Kid put one knee on the ground and rested his gun on the other, pointing upward. His heart and pulse were steady, but he couldn't see his nose in front of his face. With perfect calm, his eyes focused on the window, he heard shuffling of hands and feet on the wall; with perfect calm, he heard the window push in; with perfect calm, he saw the window open, and, with help of a wisp of moonlight, he watched a bare foot and leg come in, and then another leg; with perfect calm, he saw a man enter, stretching his neck out in an effort to see in the dark. But as soon as the man took his first step, the Kid's calm evaporated like a candle blown out. He jerked up, and the impulse to aim the gun paralyzed him.

Immobilized, stiff, for a moment he didn't know what happened to him.

The intruder jumped like a hare toward the trapeze of sacks, pulling one along after him. With the same quickness, hunched down behind the wheat pile, he began to grab handfuls and toss them into his bag, secured between his feet; he kept repeating the rapid motion with great dexterity: wheat into the bag.

Four steps away, protected by darkness, the Kid watched with fixed gaze, shotgun aimed, his calm regained once again.

Suddenly it was pitch dark again as a cloud passed before the moon. The intruder let out a low curse, but at that second, he felt himself thrown to the ground, embedded among the floor tiles. He found a foot on his belly and a gun in his chest.

The lamp gaped open as if startled; in its blurred point of light, the two brothers stared at each other, both white as the wall.

"Thief! Highwayman!" shouted one.

The other spit out a horrible curse.

"Here's where I'm going to end your days!"

"Good! Finish me off!"

The intruder raised his head like a serpent and twisted his spine, grabbing the gun by the barrel: his boozy breath gave him a fierce energy.

"Finish me off, go ahead! . . . If you don't, someone else will . . . I can't help it!"

That miserable howl, the sincere confession of a born criminal who feels pulled toward crime by irresistible, ancestral forces, suddenly disarmed the Kid. He removed his foot and raised the gun barrel, passing his frozen hand over his burning forehead, and stopped, stunned as if hit by a hammer. He could hear the words of the sinner, resounding: "Have mercy on him . . . he is not to blame for the dishonor that has befallen our household."

Seeing himself free, the younger brother got up on his knees, brushing off his shirt mechanically, and with total calm he stared at the Kid as his voice, raspy from too much drink, repeated:

"Go ahead and shoot me! You caught me, what are you waiting for?"

The Kid turned his face away, like someone backing up from a precipice.

"You're my father's son, and I can't kill you . . . but go away from here, get out of here right now, and . . . may God forgive you!"

Neither spoke another word, but as soon as the intruder was gone and the Kid found himself alone in that dark granary that held his whole fortune, he bit his lips desperately, squeezed his head between his hands and started sobbing like a baby.

The little flame, yellow as gold and completely steady, gazed at him through the blurred glass of the lamp, as if it were an eye alive with intelligence.

THE CRAVING

Amidst the reddish tints of sunset, a delirium of brilliant colors, she walked along serenely, relaxed, with solemn majesty, like a great goddess of the countryside. Her bosom, full of vitality, swayed softly with the harmonious rhythm of a classic poem, and at the bodice, full breasts suggested themselves like ivory marvels, while around her face, white and solid as a tender almond, light hair emerged, the color of ripe wheat, forming a golden halo. She bore a basket on her head which, like the crown of a prosperous empire, seemed made not of bits of straw but of strands of woven gold. From inside the basket shone a treasure of lively colors, the first fruit of the season, the first divine greeting of spring.

She was on her way back from a little orchard of dark earth with the season's earliest offering, full of the voluptuous joy of a gardener picking the best blossoms to make a pretty and promising bouquet. Still astir from the effort, her nostrils trembled, and a little humidity covered her mother-of-pearl face.

Her gait was serene and relaxed as she ambled along paths with no mysteries or surprises, confident that a tranquil peace would be her pleasant companion.

Under the jeweled colors of the sky, she seemed a proud flower about to open and bear fruit. But alas, she was a bloom with a little worm gnawing inside the calyx, for the fruit announced by that vigorous, healthy branch never took form. In the town, they called her the Barrenness, because ten years had passed since her wedding and her womb was still as empty as a virgin's. Love had taken hold of her like a deity that brings joy with its presence but gives no gifts; it had made her a wife, but not a mother. Her husband, a goodly fellow from solid earth, was enchanted by his love for her—too much, maybe, according to the neighborhood women who peeked from doors ajar as the two embraced or kissed in their shady cellar. But the couple only thought of loving each other like a pair of turtledoves as time went on, until one day, they suddenly noticed something they hadn't thought of before. They had no children! They looked at each other, surprised, as if asking for a reason for such an absurd thing, but since they didn't know the answer, they both remained silent.

But if up until then they hadn't known what an infinite longing was, from that day on they became all too aware. Their pure joy of loving each other just because they did became mixed with a new desire: the wish that the love they felt for one another should also bear the promised fruit.

Now it was more than merely an unconscious yearning for each other's lips; it became a certain pleasing hope for a new, more serene blessing. The thought of a child brought them together often, like a mysterious current, and while she turned red, he, trembling and pale, looked at her with humble tenderness, as if about to offer up a prayer to her; as if revering her charms would lead to a yet unborn charm . . . And they waited anxiously, their happiness accompanied by a shaky confidence, for the great event.

But as a year passed, and then another, without the slightest sign, husband and wife became impatient, and anxiety took hold of them: their yearning started to concentrate into a stubborn obsession. At that point, the townspeople could sniff out the drama, and with the perverse instincts of lower beings, they dug their clutches into the weakest spot: now the two of them together were referred to as the Barrens, a nickname to announce their misfortune.

On his forehead, a deep furrow of visible anger formed, and a glimpse of longing melancholy appeared in her serene eyes, suggesting sparks of sadness.

But hope lingered on, encouraged by their young, healthy bodies that seemed to offer the best token of future promise.

After all, didn't lots of imperfect beings have children, and lovely ones at that? Why, then, couldn't they, as robust as they were, have a little nest of angels with soft bottoms and eyes as bright as pretty candles?

But alas, those fine spouses didn't realize that in human gardens, as among plants, the showiest sprout may not be the one to bear fruit . . . perhaps because of too much sap. The excess in beauty might be lost in the bearing, and the most luxurious love could be sterile.

And so as month followed month without even the first chick appearing in that nest, the sacred hope, caressed by so much desire, slowly took on the appearance of a plume of smoke that hadn't produced a single spark.

Once again what seemed so sure to be came to nothing; once again, in dream's garden, a bud had lost its petals without ever having blossomed into a rose.

After ten years of matrimony, then, they still loved each other with the same goodwill and constancy, but without anxiety or delirium. Their deep, unchangeable affection was that of two companions going together along the same road, destined to share a common fate, whether good or bad. They had resigned themselves, and as their tranquil gazes met, the old fever was gone; they no longer wondered, "Who knows? Maybe, finally . . ." But that wrinkle stayed upon his brow, the mark of a day of anxiety, and in her serene eyes, a bit of longing nostalgia remained, refining and ennobling her features. Together they inherited that indivisible legacy, the poisonous nickname: the Barrens.

And so the good wife returned from the orchard that day, crowned with a cornucopia of dazzling spring fruit and a laugh at her lips. She arrived with the lingering smile of a sweetheart who doesn't forget her beloved no matter how far away he is, and she spread the gift out on the table, saying, "Look how splendid! I brought it just for you to taste . . ." And she walked on, calm and serene like a great country goddess. The fantastic outburst of the sunset tinged her with purple light, like blood from an imaginary slaughter; her arms were firm and graceful like marble columns, with a face to match.

She went out to the pomegranates planted on a little slope, and was surprised to feel that squeeze in her heart and moment of anxiety like the one that had hit her on the way that morning, that had stayed with her a good part of the afternoon while she was tying up the young bean stalks and watering the garden, row by row.

Except that now, whatever it was, seemed more alive: like a blinding, a shiver, an enchantment that paralyzed her as she dug her feet into the earth and her eyes stared

40

at the trees, clumped together in a little group like guards stopped at the edge of a plain.

The sun was waning, with its last luxurious beams still illuminating the sky like wisps of a faraway fire, sprinkling the stand of pomegranates with reddish and purple flecks. She thought they looked the same as a few days earlier, when they were still blushed with their rosy blossoms; except that now not a single flower remained. In their place were little baby pomegranates, just like miniature crowns on dolls' heads, all trimmed and pretty.

Oh, those little tiny fruits! It was indeed a magical sunset!

Feeling the evening overtake her, eager as bad news, among the sounds of crickets and of mystery, she took a step forward . . . but that immense yearning made her turn back again, and her eyes, full of longing like a lamb's gaze, filled with tears. Crazed tears, gushing out not from any known sorrow but from a frightening melancholy without limits. She took a step back, and another, into the grove . . . but, suddenly scared, she fled the temptation that obsessed her and ran like a child terrified by the monsters of a fairy tale.

She held on to the basket made of strands of gold woven together, her white face showing one disturbed look after another.

When she reached the paths of the outskirts of town, she slowed her pace, all sweaty and nervous.

She met men and women returning from the fields with bundles on their backs: they all greeted her lazily, after having worked for hours in the hot sun. She didn't even respond, for fear of bursting into tears, and to avoid that she bit her full lips, red as cherries.

She made her way forward clumsily, concentrating on getting to her house. As soon as she crossed the threshold, she set the basket on the floor and collapsed into an armchair. Her husband heard her and came out of the kitchen with a smile on his lips.

"You're so late! I got supper ready while I was waiting for you . . . "

"Ah, God will reward you, my dear! If you only knew . . . "

She let the rays of goodness from that greeting revive her, and she hurried to set the table. They sat down, but as soon as she raised the soup spoon to her mouth, that thought of the pomegranates came back to wound her maliciously, like a great whip. Those little tiny pomegranates, just now emerging from the diapers of those blossoms.

She pushed the plate away with distaste, and, bursting into sobs, she ran upstairs like a crazed spirit.

The man, frozen by surprise, sat for a moment with his mouth agape, then ran upstairs after her. He found her in the bedroom with her head on the bed, weeping disconsolately. He raised up her head carefully, looking into her face . . . Then, incapable of holding back or hiding her anxiety, she held him tight, so tight she was choking him, and confessed everything, finishing up slowly, as if in a dream.

"I know it can't be so . . . but . . . I'd almost say that I must be . . . that this is a real craving!"

Her husband jumped up as if a slingshot had hit his heart. With no color in his lips and startled eyes, he stared at her, and then let out a great yell like a hoarse organ. He raised her up in his arms and pulled her onto the bed as delicately as a feather. Drowning her in a river of kisses, he buried his head in her chest to hide two burning tears. He had only cried one other time since his adulthood: the day he lost his mother.

He undressed her slowly, with profound respect, as if she were a sacred idol, kissing her bare feet and then softly covering her up. Finally, he murmured in her ear:

"Don't move, I'll be right back."

Smiling mysteriously, he clambered down the stairs.

Upon that Olot bed,[1] with flowers and angels at the head, the woman waited, half-raised, her eyes shining behind her swollen eyelids, her cheeks burning; she waited

---

[1] Olot is a small manufacturing town in the province of Girona.

with racing heart, concentrating her whole being on that long-yearned-for wait.

A quarter of an hour passed, a little bit more . . .

Suddenly the stairway thundered with happy noise, and he came in, panting from the crazy run, and without saying a word, he spread his offering on the bed: a green cascade of little painted heads, crowns trimmed: each one bounced with a gleam of the oil lamp like a bursting of new life.

The new mother straightened up anxiously, all her nerves on edge, stared with resplendent eyes, drunk with desire, and passionately sunk her hands into the pile of little pomegranates.

She started to nibble one after another of those green, sour fruits with strange delight, with crazy impulse; so acidic she had to grimace. God knows how many she ate! Finally, exhausted, her head fell back on the pillow and her arms gave out, languishing by her sides.

Meanwhile, the goodly fellow from solid earth, ecstatic, mute, contemplated her with mouth agape and a great gaze, rendered dumb from emotion. It was the gaze with which one stares at something that takes one's heart, without understanding; the great mysteries that may engender either Happiness or Misfortune.

ACCEPTANCE

The bells tolled slowly, plaintively, with spaced-out, sad rings that filled hearts with anxiety. The ringer must have been an artist who knew how to stir up the embers of love inside every soul, even the most parched, to spark a little flame of brotherly sentiment and compassion.

Around the entryway, seated on chairs lined up against the wall, out of the way, were the women, still, arms crossed, in withdrawn postures, with expressions of great grief, eyelids fallen and brows raised. They looked like a mysterious guard of murmuring statues, following the rosary recited with wholesome voice by the hired woman who presided over the scene from the far end of the wall facing the street.

An oil lamp hung from a corner of the wall, blinking sadly, like a sick person's eye, moving the nervous shadows around, by dint of its rusty light, thus creating great curtains of black gauze to dress the whole room in mourning.

Inside the kitchen, completely dark, the family huddled together, distractedly echoing the monotonous murmur from the entry.

"Our Father, who art in heaven," the hired woman was reciting in a pitiful tone devoid of inflections.

"Give us this day our daily bread," the chorus of grieving statues responded softly.

"Our daily bread," echoed the muffled voices coming from the dark kitchen.

The sound of tinkling rosaries mingled with the parish bells . . . ding dong, ding dong . . . vibrating over the town and spreading into the peaceful evening their plaint for the dead.

Suddenly, Grandfather, the widower, got up noiselessly from among his family, as if his feet weren't touching the floor, and went upstairs. His last step made the wooden step creak.

"Someone's going upstairs," gasped the daughter-in-law with a shudder.

"It's father," responded the son, barely perceptible.

And they continued the prayer.

Upstairs, a feeble light gleamed through the door to the hall: it came from the dead woman's room.

Grandfather, the widower, went into the room, arms hanging down, head on his chest. From the red rim of his cap, worn backwards, some whitish hair stuck out like tufts of hemp. A black wool scarf twisted around his neck and chin; under the sweater, his chest seemed more sunken than usual and his back more humped.

He approached the bed slowly, shuffling his feet as if he couldn't quite get them to move along. The deceased lay on fresh sheets, stiff in her black attire, arms extended, with yellowed hands, the color of unpolished brass, crossed over her stomach. A rosary of shell beads hung from her fingers; its faded blue tassels had slipped toward her left hip and draped there, tangled and sprawled out like a wig of one thrown off a cliff. Her head lay flat on the bed, the forehead lower than the chin, adorned by a black handkerchief with another of color placed around her jaws and tied at the top, to keep her mouth from gaping open. That mouth, closed by force, formed a long pleat across her face, with lips tucked inwards, sucked by the vacuum left by gums with no teeth. Above, the pleat of her nose, sharp as a bird's beak, showed the wide-open nostrils, long and black. Her feet were covered only by linen stockings, with the soles pulled together, flat and gloomy, like hands held up to stop those who would enter.

In spite of the air coming through the wide-open window, like the breath of a quiet monster, the room held an odd odor, the ether of the sick person's final medication mixed with candle wax from the last sacraments. An oil lamp in a small plate on a little table by the door sputtered once in a while, as if there were salt in the wick. Next to the plate, keeping the lamp company, were the shoes of the deceased. They hadn't put them on her because that was bad luck: the dead who wear shoes to the cemetery bring another family member along with them within a year's time.

Grandfather, the widower, paused at the head of the bed; his eyes were dry like two pieces of blurred glass; his hands, gnarled and hardened like an owl's claws, trembled at his side with that chronic shaking that made him useless for any sort of task. He raised his head slowly and gazed at the deceased: he hadn't looked straight at her like that, by voluntary impulse, for over twenty years. He stared at her, but it was as if staring at something he didn't recognize and didn't want to know. His gaze was dull, cold, deader than the cadaver itself. He saw a smooth forehead with taut skin, as if stuck onto the bone; the thin, stunted neck, yellowing between the bodice and handkerchiefs like a flap of rancid fat. Grandfather, the widower, felt a sensation of strangeness prying its way inside him, making him feel that the stiffened woman in that bed was not the same woman to whom he'd been married for so many years; puzzled by that odd sensation, he kept on staring at the corpse as if his own pupils had also stopped forever beneath his eyelids.

In the meantime, laments from below continued wafting through the dark throat of the open window:

"Our Father who art in heaven . . ."

"Ding dong! Ding dong!"

". . . forgive us our trespasses as we forgive those . . ."

And from the stairwell the soft echoing murmur arose from the kitchen:

". . . as we forgive those . . . who trespass against us . . ."

Suddenly, a thought flashed through the thick quiet of Grandfather's brain, like a moonbeam penetrating a primitive forest. It occurred to him that those funeral bells would be ringing again soon enough, and those unmoving women would return to pray the rosary at the entryway. But then, he wouldn't hear it: he would be the stiff one, laid out on the marriage bed, right where his wife was now. The thought was clear, light, clean; it left Grandfather serene and tranquil as if it hadn't passed through his brain at all, as if he hadn't seen a thing. His heartbeat, irregular and weak like a worn-out machine, did not change, nor did a single tear moisten the blurred glass of his eyes. He knew he was old, and that the old have to let go of life, just as overripe fruit lets go of the branch and falls to the ground. It was natural, and what was natural held no terror for Grandfather. Every companion of his time, male and female, who had "gone away" seemed to show him the way, signaling him to follow, and he was ready to do so without being coaxed. After all, "What can I do in this world?" he said to himself. In his time, he had done his duty as a man, but now he couldn't hold hoe or pruner, and his son and daughter-in-law had been running the household for some time; they barely had room for their little ones. It was up to him, then, to make room for them: the room he was in begged for new occupants, and he would let them have it gladly. Now, besides his companions, his wife was calling to him as well, from up there. She held out her hand to help him cross over from one world to the other. Do it soon, the sooner the better! . . . Grandfather looked at his dead wife as if to pass on to her that secret desire, hidden behind his glazed, fixed eyes. Suddenly he was struck by the fear that she would forget about him and leave him all alone upon the earth, and it inspired him to give her a reminder.

Slowly, shuffling as if his feet had trouble following him, with his head lowered down into his sunken chest and his back more humped than ever, he moved from the bed to the little table, reaching out with his trembling hands. It seemed that, aware of the old man's effort, the two velvet shoes, paired in such a brotherly fashion and moved by a mysterious impulse, advanced in order to help him in his task.

Grandfather took hold of them and returned to the bed, and by the light of the lamp, sputtering as if it had salt in the wick, he serenely, tranquilly, placed the shoes on the stiff feet of the dead woman.

From the dark throat of the window, the last, muffled syllables of the rosary entered, and along with them the desolate ding-dong of the bells.

SILENT SOULS

The Peró and Xuriguer families had adjacent fields, and from that proximity, quarrels had been born years ago. To find out who had priority over the road that separated the two fields, the great-grandfathers had disputed bitterly and had gone to court, spending everything they had on lawsuits, only to end up with the road evenly divided, as it had always been. In addition to that access, they also shared a ferocious hatred that ended up being passed on from generation to generation, not to be placated by time or retaliations. Those Capulets and Montagues in the garb of Catalan peasants did not go so far as to spill blood over their differences, but they kindled their own blood more than once.

Things went more or less like so: one fine day, the Xuriguers would find their melons smashed to bits in their own field; the melons' owner, while raging inside, said not a word that might jeopardize him, but a few days later a certain mysterious wind would carry the neighbors' sheafs off into the ditch, which pulled them dutifully downstream. The owner of the lost sheafs would contemplate the spoiled harvest and contain within him a crazed laugh, completely silent. But before too long some buckshot, fired from who knows where, would catch a distracted Xuriguer off guard, leaving his hip looking like a leather sieve. That would be followed by a rock from a slingshot hitting the youngest Peró girl in the eye while she was peacefully tending the piglets, rendering her one-eyed forever.

Of course everyone figured where the buckshot and the rock had come from, but they all kept it to themselves, according to a fraternal philosophy that it was no skin off their teeth, and if those neighbors wanted to make their beds that way, then they could lie in them as well.

And so that beastly rancor continued for years and decades and would have gone on indefinitely had not the usual arranger of things stepped in.

Both families were in dire straits as a result of so many lawsuits, neither one having been able to keep their former holdings and both reduced to the simple plot that had caused all the disputes, eternally separated by the ominous road between them. And since there was nothing else, Perós and Xuriguers had to spend their lives working side by side from sunup to sundown scratching the ground to coax out their daily bread. Spying and eyeing each other continually, the young man Peró happened to notice the young lady Xuriguer—Xurie, they mockingly called her. Without meaning to, he saw that she worked like a young filly and whistled better than any blackbird even if she whistled to annoy him. For her part, she admitted to herself that if Peró weren't who he was, and if he hadn't put on such a mocking face when he looked her way, he could have been a good-looking fellow who might turn the head of any young lady.

From the moment she made such a confession to herself, convinced that she was doing it to annoy the young man, she kept on warbling happily with the contagious joy of a bird on the first day of spring. In return, he laughed to himself as he listened; the little giggle escaped on its own, and he would have sworn that it was in devilish mockery. The furtive glances that had crossed between them before became more frequent, but still very askance and sly, as if they felt guilty for not keeping the old, traditional hatred alive.

At that point the draft came along and the young Peró got an unlucky number. A gossipy neighbor hurried off to the Xuriguers' house to give them the news:

"Haven't you heard? Young Peró drew the black card!"

The Xuriguer parents were delighted; but the girl went all white as if she'd been grief-struck. She went to work the field all alone, forgetting to whistle her tune, but busting up the clumps of dirt ferociously, making them jump and fly like evil spirits. Then when it came time for a rest and a snack, instead of sitting at the far edge of the field as usual, she wandered over toward the road and sat down at the peak of the boundary. Peró, just on the other side, surprised, stopped to look at her; their eyes met; both turned a lively red and lowered their heads quickly; then each one began eating their respective lunches.

From that day on, whenever they coincided in their fields, the same thing happened: a quick glance, faces as red as cherries, and two silent lunches.

Days and months went on like that. Then she came down with typhus and was sent to bed; he was called up by the government. He left and spent more than three years away; she recovered, after passing the disease on to her father, who died from it.

When the young Peró returned from the service, he learned that the young Xuriguer was married and had children: since there was no man in the household, her mother wouldn't leave her in peace until she brought one home. At that point, Peró discovered that his town was ugly, and if it hadn't been for fear of the townspeople's gossip, he'd have returned to serve the king again.

The first time that the two neighbors saw each other in their respective fields after the long absence, they didn't even dare glance at each other, as if a barrier even greater than the old one had sprung up between them. Even so, after a period of vacillation, instinct was stronger than shame and they gazed at one another, scared, with the most desolate feeling of disbelief. She thought he had come back all skinny and yellow, and his face was that of an outsider. He noticed that she was in tatters and barefoot, and that her pregnancy completely disfigured her. But just as three years ago, after that gaze they both turned red and lowered their heads, confused.

Peró's mother, seeing that she was getting old, kept an eye peeled for a daughter-in-law. Peró wasn't very interested in marrying, but they did need another woman in the house, and so he brought in the one his mother liked best.

And so, years passed, many years . . .

There wasn't much talk in the town anymore about the feud between Perós and Xuriguers; the legend only interested the old ladies now, except that once in a while, the elderly one-eyed Peró woman, remembering the old days, would say with rancor in her voice:

"If that shitty nephew[2] of mine had blood in his veins, they'd have paid dearly for the eye I lost!"

The old ladies of the town agreed with her and lamented that "that shitty nephew" was just a loser who wasn't good for a damn thing.

------

[2] The expression "cagai del nebot" is just as vulgar in Catalan as "shitty nephew" is in English.

But Peró wasn't aware of those opinions, or at least he pretended not to be. A hard worker and a peaceful sort, he spent all day, every day, in the field, silently glancing toward the neighbors any time it seemed she was around. She was always in tatters and barefoot, always pregnant with one beastly pregnancy after another, like an animal bought to bring cubs into the world or a hired cow. She would do the same: the poor defeathered blackbird had no desire to sing, but she still reacted to the silent call, and her eyes, filled with a great, tired sadness, often looked toward the neighbors' place without her even realizing it.

And so, always attracted by a secret sympathy and always dragged down by the strange silence of their souls, those two beings, so close and yet so far apart, just like their two fields, approached old age without ever having exchanged anything more than glances filled with shame.

Perhaps they never would have realized that they truly loved one another, that they went together like ox and yoke, as the peasants would say. Like yoked oxen, they went along with their heads bowed, seeing only the furrow they were opening, without dreams or illusions.

Then the rumor started running through town that there was a great struggle going on in the Xuriguer household. People didn't think much of Xuriguer's husband. Stingy and mean, he hadn't brought anything into the marriage but the clothes on his back, and when he realized that his wife was losing strength, due to hard work and bringing children into the world like a beast of burden, he began to worry that she would pass on, leaving nothing for him. He would be at the mercy of the oldest son, and he began to complain and snarl that she should insure him by leaving him the property. But since she had hated him for years for his bad temper and meanness, she got stubborn and refused to sign any papers, as a way of revenge. The fighting started, worsening her precarious health and ending up in an illness that left her cheeks and eyes sunken, legs skinny and weak, belly inflated with dropsy, a sort of last, fruitless pregnancy that kept her sides bulging, in one of destiny's terrible ironies.

She knew she couldn't last much longer.

"The land is calling me," she would say to the townswomen. And to be ready to reintegrate herself into it at any moment, she used her waning strength to go out and take her leave of the things she loved.

She set out for the field, where she hadn't gone for some time, on a lovely October afternoon, with birds singing and the last summer warmth settling on the dark, empty land. Old Peró, no one called him young anymore, saw her slowly crossing the road, panting and struggling. He was startled: he barely recognized her, so changed she was. He leaned his gnarled hands on the pitchfork handle and straightened up his back, curved over toward the earth after half a century of working it, and gazed for a long, long while . . .

When he took up his tool and returned to the task, his eyes were red, and something like a stubborn animal gnawed at him from inside. Just as, years before, his neighbor had attacked the clumps of earth with a fury to make evil spirits jump and fly, not knowing how to dispel the muffled rumbling of a great grief, he succumbed to the same frenzy now.

When he raised his head once again, he saw that her worthless husband was there too. She was seated, sheltered, on the boundary, and he was next to her, gesticulating and red-faced like a partridge, waving his arms about and stomping on the ground more than digging in the earth. Old Peró again propped himself up on his pitchfork handle.

"It's a good bet they're talking about the inheritance," he said to himself. "Judas's blood! When he can see she's more in the other world than in this one!"

Flooded with pity and tenderness, he could no longer keep his eyes off the field next door. His neighbor kept on arguing, and she let her head drop to her chest, yellow as a corpse, without answering or even moving, as if she didn't hear him. Suddenly old Peró felt like a bullet had hit him in the chest, a red fury blinded his eyes, he dropped his pitchfork, and then . . .

Not even he could have explained what happened next, what mysterious force launched him into the neighbors' land. All he knew was that in a flash he found himself crushing the man in his arms and foaming with rage.

"Pig, worse than a pig, to strike your wife!!!"

The two old-timers were white with rage, trembling from head to foot; they stared at each other for a full minute: one openmouthed with surprise, his eyes wide and stupid like a fish; the other, enraged, fixing his own eyes on his rival like burning arrows. When he got hold of himself and recovered his speech, old Peró bowed his head like an animal about to attack, and, threatening the other with his pitchfork grasped firmly in his spread-out fingers, he growled lowly:

"If you ever touch her again, even with the edge of your fingernail, I'll tear you apart from top to bottom. As God is my witness!"

He turned away to leave. Then he glanced at the woman. She was immobile, her hands grasped together with fear, waxen lips, staring at the two of them, terrified. Peró was startled, assailed by a moment of doubt. Then he suddenly jumped back to his own field and crossed it with long strides, as if he were being pursued. She covered her face with her hands and let out a long sobbing wail.

Old man Peró and old woman Xuriguer passed on to the other world without ever having exchanged a single word.

CARNIVAL

The Marquise of Artigues was all alone in her usual place, her eternal place, behind the balcony windows, sunken into the armchair with a little table in front of her, hand-held glasses at her fingers, and a woolen shawl over her dry, bony shoulders.

The young servants had all gone with the doorkeeper to watch the arrival of the people attending a great masked ball that was the topic of all conversations the last few days. The butler joined them as well, and Gloria, the older maid, after settling the lady in comfortably, retired prudently, taking the oil lamp with her so that the lady could say her daily devotions undisturbed.

The Marquise, stuck in place by the immobility forced on her by paralysis, remained still in the room left in shadows when the maid left.

The newspaper on the table caught a bit of light, and a little more filtered through the half-open blinds, emanating from lamps on the Avenue. The beam first struck the Marquise's head, vigorously accentuating her features of an old Roman senator; then it continued in its path, painting a strip of ceiling and wall with golden tones. The interior of the alcove was full of shadow and mystery, like the entrance to a mausoleum. The furniture, sparse and severe, was of an earlier time; placed along the edges of the room, the pieces seemed beastly prisoners of the darkness.

Her litany of daily prayers finished, the Marquise slowly let the rosary beads and hands drop to her lap, and she glanced at the street distractedly. Not many passersby were on the Avenue at that hour, and those who walked by were wearing their normal clothes.

"Thank God!" the lady thought to herself. Her face, lit as in a Rembrandt painting in the darkened room, showed a glimmer. It was Mardi Gras, and for the last three days she had seen nothing but disguises. She was sick and tired of the banal spectacle.

She had little to distract her on those long evenings of solitude and immobility other than the newspaper and a prayer book, with no more company than an occasional parasitic beggar or some old friend as full of years and ailments as she was herself, who would always repeat the same things told in the same words. The poor woman, impatient and restless, longing for something new and stimulating, had looked forward to the revelers of Mardi

Gras passing beneath her balcony, cheering things up with their laughter and merrymaking. But when it came, with its loud screams, crazy clamor, parades of unkempt ne'er-do-wells telling offensive jokes and making obscene gestures . . . she felt condemned to witness the whole unruly spectacle from dawn to dusk, the stupid and libidinous scene of hysterical dreams. Her polished, aristocratic taste took offense; it was more than her hardened, vestal modesty could bear; simply too much for the methodical stillness of an elderly, ailing woman.

At that point, the proud impatience of a person used to being obeyed rebelled, and she ordered the windows closed to that profane, desecrating street scene. Stuck in her invalid's cart, she had herself wheeled to the rear of the house, away from the vociferous brouhaha from below. But even there she could hear the debauchery as it attacked her ears, setting her thoughts in turmoil, and finally, tiring of gazing at sad walls and the silent servants surrounding her, she yearned once again for light, movement, life, and her cart would roll slowly, softly over the rugs to return to the alcove. The windows and blinds were reopened; the sunken armchair again received the ungainly body; the table was set in front of her once more, like a bridge with four buttresses covering her useless legs; and her ashen eyes moved nervously beneath the crystal of her glasses held up with a handle.

And so the Marquise awaited the next crisis of sadness and boredom. In fact, that very evening she experienced one that was exceptional for its unexpected consequences.

It all started when she complained that the lamp wasn't burning right and she asked that others be brought, one after another, until she had tried all the hand lamps in the house — sending each one away, saying that they weren't arranged well, that everyone was conspiring against her to make her life all the more desperate. The butler, an amateur archaeologist, tried to calm her down, and she sent him away, grumbling that if he took care of what he was supposed to instead of buying moth-eaten pieces of junk, these things wouldn't happen. She bawled the cook out for serving her old stale broth, made a month ago; she threatened to fire the young maid for talking back. She accused Gloria, the senior maid, of being a hypocrite and only doing things to suit herself.

"If only I could take care of myself! If only God hadn't sent me this terrible punishment! You wouldn't be in my sight for another second!" Frenetic, exasperated, she nervously tapped her horn-rimmed glasses on her bony, skinny legs. Her voice trembled with sorrow and indignation, and then stopped as two tears ran down her face and filled her mouth with bitter salt.

The noble beast showed no signs of calming down until she heard a low, intermittent noise behind her, which seemed her own echo. She turned her head: curled up in a corner, Gloria was fighting off violent sobs with her head buried in her wrinkled apron. As the Marquise let her tormented gaze fall upon Gloria, she felt all her functions stop, and her head fell, her arms became still, her mouth opened, and her stare fixed itself upon the maid . . . But that only lasted a moment. She turned back around as if she hadn't noticed anything, and, exhaling her despotic pride from every feature of her authoritarian face, she looked at the butler and the young servants surrounding her with disconcerted glances, and she brusquely sent them all away.

"Go on, go to the kitchen . . . what are you doing here? Let's see if at least I can have supper tonight . . . And you, Don Joan, write that letter to the farmer right now and tell him he sent me stale eggs . . . Everyone takes advantage of me . . ."

The servants vanished in a flash, sighing with relief, for they knew the storm was waning. The lady let a minute go by, and then, with a very different tone of voice, she called for Gloria, but the maid, with her face buried in her apron, didn't hear, or couldn't respond.

"She's pouting!" the Marquise thought, worried. She repeated the call, a bit more imperiously: "Gloria, are you deaf?"

"What would you like, Madame?" Gloria quickly answered, her voice nasal from crying.

"Bring me a handkerchief, I dropped mine."

Gloria left the alcove, and when she returned and the lady saw her holding back tears and turning her face away to hide them, she felt all malice from a moment ago fading away like a drop of water on blotting paper, and she exclaimed with false seriousness:

"Come on, now, what are you bawling about? You're getting very strange, Gloria."

The maid ceased her respectful holding back and, falling at the knees of the Marquise, she took her hand and covered it with kisses and tears.

"Forgive me, Madame, my dear Madame."

The Roman senator's head turned quickly away from the beam of light, and a voice broken by emotion emerged from the darkness:

"But . . . what's this about . . . dear?"

"Please forgive me, Madame, I'd rather die than provoke your anger, and yet it seems I always make you angry . . ."

The Marquise tried to say something. Her lips and chin trembled, her misty eyes shone from the recess of her shadowy shelter, but no words came out. She was well acquainted with the great meekness that often unintentionally humiliated her own headstrong pride, making her aware of her unjust whims. This time she was even more taken aback; she wanted to cry of shame, to ask for pardon herself, to draw that innocent head raised and imploring toward her, but . . . she didn't dare. On the one hand, class pride tyrannized her, and on the other, the stifling shrinking away of an old virgin who never learned how to love when she was young put a clamp on her mouth and kept her from reaching out her arms. But the effort to hold herself back was so strong that it completely upset her, and when she finally could talk, her voice came out harsh and toneless, like some men's voices; a strange one she didn't know and that the maid hardly recognized.

The Marquise said: "Yes, yes, you do make me mad . . . when you . . . do things . . . like that."

A new flood of kisses and tears fell upon her hand.

"Because you know you mustn't let yourself get upset . . ."

"My dear Madame! . . . My dear Madame!"

"What will your doctor say when he sees you tomorrow, all out of sorts?"

"That doesn't matter, as long as he doesn't find you out of sorts!"

The intimate pain of that response sounded so sincere that it went straight to the lady's deepest feelings, bursting through all laws of pride and inhibition. Before she knew what she was doing, the Marquise of Artigues took hold of her companion's head and pulled it to her bosom. They held that embrace for a time, one drowning in a rough tenderness, the other dying of happiness.

In all the years they had been together, this was the first time they had manifested the mutual affection they both held, clearly, without reservation. As if that embrace constituted the definitive revelation, they both felt that the other one was a necessity, as if their two incomplete lives had melted into one.

Not another word was said. Gloria brought in her dinner, as she did every day, and served it on the little table without daring to raise her eyes, full of infinite strangeness. The Marquise, for her part, ate quietly and felt her heart uplifted by an unknown force.

The other servants, sensing harmony from afar, asked Gloria if she wanted to go out and see the costumes, and the butler said he would take a walk. Gloria, sharing the lady's pardon with the others, stayed behind and closed the door after them. The two women remained alone in the house, and felt a secret peace of intimacy, a great happiness without exchanging a word.

The maid brought in the lady's rosary so she could say her prayers, and quietly withdrew, removing the lamp as she went, since the lady always said her devotions in the dark, illuminated only by the Avenue lights, dimmed by the distance. Gloria went to say her own prayers, a great wordless oration full of loving balm toward everything on earth and in heaven, a silent prayer of happiness.

Gloria was forty-five, and thirty of those years had been
spent in the lady's service; she was still a girl when she began the job, and she had become a woman without even
noticing, nor had she noticed that she had left her barren
youth behind. She was suddenly middle-aged without love,
liberty, a nest, or anything of her own except for a great devotion, like a faithful dog or a voluntary slave to the lady.
It was the chain that had defined the conscience and will
of all her family, the stamp that the House of Artigues had
left on the backs of generations of men, vassals, farmers,
lackeys. The heritage had penetrated the soul of that poor,
humble being who never came to grips with who she was,
as if her only destiny had been to annihilate herself to give
weight to another, and she accepted that sacrifice with the
resignation of one who has taken on an unknown oath or
a remote atonement.

Since she had entered the Marquise's service — who at
the time wasn't Marquise but daughter of the Marquis —
she hadn't thought about or lived for anything but the
lady. The noblewoman was twenty years her senior, and
she was a strong woman, bold and brave like an Amazon
warrior. Ugly and full of pride but not vanity, knowing
well that she did not have the character for the joys and
servitude of either married or religious life, she refused to
marry or enter a convent, remaining the family spinster,

while she still had a family. Motherless, she went through
Europe with her father and brothers for years with the
ambulatory passion characteristic of her lineage. In Paris
she witnessed her older brother's death from falling off
a horse; in Geneva, a pleurisy took her father; her little
brother died in Valencia from some common illness. Alone
in the world, her soul virilized and strengthened by pain
and solitude, she was goaded on by the atavistic, poisonous impulse and decided to abandon the cemetery of
memories that the old world represented for her and go
on to the new world to await the solemn arrival of old
age, not too far off. But an unforeseen event, a white tu-
mor that settled in her knee, changed all those plans, and
she had to stay in Barcelona, which she was never again to
leave except to have her bones taken to the faraway family property. From then on, her nature, which had been
so strong and firm, suffered one ailment after another, as
if to settle the score with all the previous activity. The cruelest was a paralysis that stopped her legs, thus burying
the boundless energy she had once known. During the
period of suffering desperation without resignation, she
began to notice the devotion of her servant. Her headstrong pride and inborn despotism drove everyone away;
doctors, servants, butlers, friends lost patience; all living
things abandoned her except the faithful dog, the voluntary slave that was Gloria, who remained right there, help-

ing her with humility, suffering with her, watching out for her mistress with sweet gazes. Hers was a tender voice, making excuses for the lady before others when the outbursts came and calming her down with affection and solicitude when the ailments or the disappointments became too great to bear. The Marquise's hardened and mummified heart, full of prejudice and scorn from her status, came to know tenderness and was revived by the sheer force of the magical effect of that devotion. Gloria's quiet heroism, devoid of any guile, raised her, in the mistress's eyes, from a little, unimportant animal to a useful servant, from favorite to absolutely necessary, to finally become something beyond definition that gets inside the soul and secretly dominates it imperceptibly. Animal selfishness had once informed the Marquise that her peace of mind was in the hands of that servant, but one day, without even renouncing egoism, the noble and just part of her soul threw off lowly yokes, and she felt the elevated company of the soul of a friend. That was when the Marquise, so long punished by pain, began to lower her proud head to divine will and accept her fate with bitter resignation. But now that she was calm and serene for having looked outside herself, she noticed that the maid, crushed under the weight of silent suffering on behalf of her lady, had become, like herself, a bundle of unconfessable pain. The Marquise spoke to the doctor, who declared that the faithful dog would die of her very faithfulness, for the suffering had affected her heart. When? When God wishes . . . Endangered lives like that one might last years, or they might end suddenly by any random sneeze. The former Amazon warrior, the proud descendent of the House of Artigues, became petrified as she listened to that terrible sentence. Struck by such a violent blow, she was defenseless and conquered by the meekest of creatures. That creature reigned from then on, with the unconscious gentleness of a sick child, without realizing it: over the other servants, the house, everything, because she reigned over her lady's heart.

"Don't contradict her, let her do what she wants," the doctor had said.

"I just want her to live!" responded the Marquise.

But while people's plans are within their wills, other passions that might break those wills are without.

As was mentioned, the Marquise was in her usual place behind the balcony windows, distractedly looking outside. Vague memories of other times passed through her aroused brain, clouds reddened by far-off rays of the sunset of her youth. Her heart, finally freed from walls of ancient prohibitions, felt lively and warm as gusts of fullness made her see the whole world differently from how she had seen it heretofore.

The Marquise of Artigues no longer felt like the woman she always thought she was; and that ruin of a firm and definite personality, instead of adding to the pain of all her other disappointments and of insisting on the waning of life that they all together produced, now brought her a joy and strength of soul unknown before.

What she could never confess, she admitted to herself now without false and silly shame; the great marvel denied by her youth, so austere and straight-laced, had come to her in old age. She loved . . . fully, strongly . . . whom? . . . What did that matter . . . a human being, another creature like herself. The object of that love wasn't what was important about the miracle, but love itself, that great warm and serene affection, that overwhelming fondness that tied her to something living and brought her out of the shadows and withered isolation in which she had been living up to now. For what ties and comforts is not that which comes from others to us but that which goes out from us to others, generously, not what is received but what is given.

Of course the Marquise of Artigues wasn't thinking all those things concretely, but she felt them with the pressing force of a great reality, and she gladly let herself give in to that sentiment without stopping to meditate on or analyze it. She was content to let herself be overtaken by a placid semiconsciousness.

Suddenly a great noise and commotion came up from the Avenue. She gazed out toward the street. It was a parade of disguised partygoers. Led by a great lantern of dazzling colors, a dozen men in pairs walked along, laughing and discreetly gesticulating. Half were dressed as Harlequin, and the other half as Pierrot—the first sporting variegated colors and ringing bells at every step, the others dressed in white satin with mimosa-colored circles as buttons and shining from head to foot as if they were covered with little mirrors.

With her turtle-shell glasses propped up on her nose, the Marquise watched them with interest. Neither their clothing nor their behavior suggested coarseness; they must have been a better class of people who were celebrating Carnival with distinction, as they should, without letting the ordinariness that reigned during those days contaminate them. They left a string of noisy kids and onlookers behind, and as the lady kept concentrating on them, she saw them arrive at the wide open door of a great house, climb a stairway covered with rugs and filled with sparkling green and gold plants, enter as a happy whirlwind into a splendid room, surrounded by exquisitely exotic women. Then she witnessed the twisting and weaving of gallant dances: pavanes, minuets, and other elegant steps of days gone by . . .

The patrician soul of the Marquise took delight in the painterly vision. Here was the beautiful, cultured Carnival, not the unworthy letting go of base instincts in the middle of the street, the venting of bad taste in front of everyone, ugly, shameful things typical of inferior classes! The Marquise returned once again to the claws of atavistic prejudices and thought that indeed there were castes preferred by God and Nature, and that only they should be in charge of the world, submitting all other disinherited castes to their control and imposing silence and obedience on them.

At that very point in her thoughts, something unexpected put an end to her reverie. Her alcove opened to a little hall, and that led to the dining room. She had just distinctly heard a groan of anguish coming from within.

The Marquise quickly turned around to face the door, and with her glasses on her nose, she tried to make out what it was through the darkness. She heard the groan again, fainter.

"Gloria!" the lady cried out, startled.

The maid's voice, feeble and altered, barely made itself heard from within the little hallway:

"Ma . . . dame . . ."

"What's wrong?"

"Oh, I don't know . . . I'm chok—"

The Roman senator's face suddenly turned yellow-green like a bronze bust, and her blood, weakened by her years, pulsated quickly through her enlarged veins.

"My dear, don't be afraid . . . It will be all right . . . ," the lady pronounced with trembling voice.

The wavering silhouette of the servant gained the threshold of the room.

"Come, come here with me!" the lady insisted affectionately.

But the silhouette advanced no further.

"What are you doing, Gloria, why don't you come?"

Another muffled, sinister groan issued forth, like a night bird, and a dull blow on the carpet indicated that a body had fallen to the floor.

The terrified lady broke out into shrieks: "Gloria, Gloria, Gloria!" The only answer to that desperate cry that seemed more a roar of the elements than a human voice was a little, husky noise from the other side of the room, sounding like a toy phonograph.

Gloria was dying. The lady was absolutely convinced of it by the cold that froze her heart. Her fingers dug into the wood of the table like claws of aged ivory, her head raised up energetically, and with an impulse of all the strength she had, she barely managed to raise herself up a little from the armchair.

"My dear! . . . I'm coming!!" she cried out to the dying woman, trying to give her courage. But her forces betrayed her and she fell back heavily into the chair. It was not until then that she fully realized her impotence. Her beloved was dying right there, at an arm's length, and she couldn't bring help or even kiss her good-bye.

The Marquise of Artigues reached out her arms, joining her twitching hands desperately, and a great sob burst forth from her throat. But suddenly the sob stopped, she brought in her arms and her knuckled fists pounded on the table. She had just felt that in life's glass, full of bile, not one more drop would fit. Her proud soul reacted, rebelling against that new and most terrible cruelty of destiny. She raised her proud head with an accusing jerk and faced the divinity, as if to demand justice. What was the reply from beyond to that mute interrogative? A mystery! All I know is that suddenly, as those eyes focused upward toward the unknown with fierce reprobation, they met with terrifying evidence. Upon the tragically convulsed face of the Marquise of Artigues, an expression of extreme stupor appeared: the desolate grimace of one who has ceased to believe.

GISELDA

As soon as they found out that the noble and powerful Viceroy of those lands was approaching, at the head of his warring troops, to teach the rebellious town a lesson for not paying its taxes, all peace-loving people fled, scattered about, from the potentate wearing silk robes embroidered with strands of gold and bearing a sword with precious jewels embedded in its hilt to the poor old-timer covered with a rough wool cape with a hood gnawed up by moths. For they all knew that the most high and powerful Lord Viceroy of those lands had a very bad temper, worse than Cain's, and it wasn't for nothing that they had given him the nickname of Hanging Post.

The name of this protagonist recalls Boccaccio's *Decameron*. The tenth tale of the tenth day features the patient Griselda, who triumphs over adversity. The two stories are quite different: the Catalan Giselda actively seeks redress, whereas the Italian Griselda simply waits for a favorable outcome. Chaucer also used a version of the story in The Clerk's Tale, and similar narrations appear elsewhere.

So, while the stragglers were hoofing it out the eastern
gates as fast as ever they could, the Lord Viceroy and his
troops entered the western gates, beating drums, bearing pendants, and waving flags, His Lordship astride his
warhorse—white as a drop of milk and haughty as a
lovely lady—completely surrounded by well-armed soldiers with their helmets glistening in the sun, mustaches
flicked up with a martial air, and hands ready on their
harquebuses.

When his lord the Viceroy arrived at city hall, he told
the mayor to give him all keys, whether to houses or prisons, for he would take charge of everything from that moment on. The mayor lowered his head and handed the keys
over to the Viceroy's lieutenant, for the mayor was more
than eighty years old and the town had no protection.

Then the Lord Viceroy asked him for what reason no
one had so much as stuck a head out the window when
he passed through the streets of the town, nor had the villagers received him with ringing bells or delegations of
artisans or barons.

And the mayor, his long white beard flowing, answered
that from that day and for the following month, the townspeople had gone on pious pilgrimages, fasting and doing
penance so that Almighty God would free them from evil
spirits. Everyone had gone, even the rector and the bell
ringers. But just as the mayor was explaining the situation,

a strange messenger dressed in black entered the room and said:

"O great and powerful Lord Viceroy, may God keep you! The noble Lady Giselda, my madame, requests humble permission to kneel at your lordship's feet."

"May your lady come!" responded the Viceroy.

The messenger left, and the noble Lady Giselda entered, as beautiful as a spring morning and as melancholy as a fall afternoon.

Her forehead glistened with the brightness of a water lily that has never seen the sun's rays, and her long mourning robes brushed along the ground like a train of pain. The powerful Viceroy was amazed.

Lady Giselda slowly advanced; she placed a knee on the ground, and her lips, fine and discolored like two rose petals, kissed the Viceroy's sinewy hand, full of scars. The noble and powerful Viceroy of those lands thought that kiss was sweeter than the sweetest preserves, and he said with a smile:

"May the gentle lady speak."

"O most powerful lord! May God bless you and bring back the love of your servants! Today the village is empty for fear of you, for it has been bruited about that you are cruel and harsh. But I have awaited your arrival."

The noble Viceroy cast a long look at the mayor.

"So that's the penance and fasting you meant, my good man?"

The mayor lowered his head, and his long beard covered his chest. Since he was more than eighty years old, he knew life was short and offered his soul to God.

The Viceroy continued: "Please go on, gentle lady."

"I alone waited for you when the villagers fled, for I have faith in your mercy and justice."

At that point the noble lady burst into sobs and her eyes filled with tears, just as dew covers blackberries at daybreak.

"O powerful lord! There was a time when the sad, sorrowful Giselda, now kneeling before you, was the happiest of women, for she had a noble and brave husband who loved her beyond anything in the world. His arms were loving sashes around her body; his eyes, mirrors of jet reflecting hers; his lips, poppies full of honey for the bees of her lips; their hearts, twin almonds not yet shelled by misfortune . . . Day and night found them always together, like the oak and its ivy, like sea and land, like body and soul. The sun shone on their good fortune, and the lads and lasses blessed them as they passed, for both of them were young, lovely, noble, and merciful . . . But O misfortune! One day the King's soldiers surrounded the house with arms flashing, and seizing husband from wife, they took him away and threw him into prison with seven locks and seven keys, seven feet below the earth . . . Just think, O powerful lord, the pain poor Giselda suffered! Taking neither food nor water, she fled through fields and woods, gorges and passes, crying her misfortune and begging birds and winds, grasses and fountains, sky and earth, to bring back her husband. When they heard her laments, the birds stopped their flight, the winds howled, the fountains wailed, the trees trembled. Sky and earth, full of tender pity, moaned for Giselda's great sorrow. Only man showed no mercy, and her husband was not returned to her. Seven years he has been imprisoned, seven years since she has laid eyes on him, seven years she has been the widow of a living man, the wife of a hanged man, seven years she has agonized, full of pain and longing. O powerful lord! Behold her here at your feet, so beaten down that she has no resemblance to the Giselda she once was. Look at her, pity her, and do justice! Return beloved to lover, husband to wife; return the mirror of jet to reflect my eyes; the poppy full of honey to my lips! Please do this, O great and powerful lord, for God will be pleased and Giselda will bless your name until the end of time!"

"Go forth, gentle lady, for I will act justly," the Viceroy said suddenly. "Leave your servant here with me and wait in your house for one hour."

"May God be with you, merciful and good Viceroy! Your words are a sweet balm upon the sad and wounded heart of Giselda . . ."

And the noble lady left, her forehead resplendent like a water lily at sunrise, but her long robes of mourning followed behind her like an endless train of sorrow.

The hour passed, and Giselda's messenger, all dressed in black, arrived in her chambers. The lady received him with a smile on her lips: "What message does the noble Viceroy send for me?"

The messenger lowered his head, his face suddenly looking sadder than the followers of a funeral procession: "The noble Viceroy sends me to tell you that tomorrow you will see the mirror of your eyes, the poppy of your lips . . ."

Giselda cried out with joy.

The messenger continued: ". . . tomorrow you will see the mirror of your eyes, the poppy of your lips, if you will sleep with him tonight."

The lady turned away as if she had been stung by a scorpion. Her forehead was as white as a lily in the moonlight, and her mourning clothes swirled around her like a black serpent.

"O messenger of outrage! I will cut out your tongue with your own knife!" she shrieked, beside herself with grief.

The messenger responded: "My tongue belongs to you, O my lady! But think, it is not my tongue that proposes such a disgrace . . ."

"Is it possible that the powerful Viceroy sent you with such a message for the noble Giselda?"

"That is what he told me to tell you. And he said more: that he requires your response within an hour."

"Oh, false and perverse man!" moaned the lady, and her neck bowed down like a lily battered by a storm.

Her ladies-in-waiting surrounded her with silver flasks full of fragrances to bring her back from her faint.

As soon as she opened her eyes full of tears, like blackberries at dawn, Lady Giselda heaved forth a great sigh. The messenger, standing stiffly by the door, heaved another.

"What are you doing here, my dear?" the lady asked.

"I await your reply, O my lady! to take it to the Viceroy."

Giselda sorrowfully exclaimed: "Can anyone have a fate darker than mine? . . . Go, hurry, my faithful servant, and tell the pervert that Giselda is of noble lineage, and even though she loves her husband more than her life, she would rather leave him in prison, closed with seven keys and seven locks, seven feet beneath the ground, than see him carry such a shame with him through the streets of the village."

The messenger left with his head held high and the happy look of a wedding party.

Lady Giselda sat by the window to contemplate her sorrows.

Within a quarter of an hour, the messenger returned with head bowed, his gaze fixed on the earth.

"What did the Viceroy say?"

"The Viceroy said that if you refuse to sleep with him tonight, at daybreak he will bring you your noble husband, my lord, to the middle of the plaza, and he will have his eyes burned out with hot irons, he will have his tongue pulled out by the torturer, he will have his hands and feet cut off with swords, and he will be drawn and quartered by four wild horses. For your noble husband, my lord, has given offense to the King and he deserves punishment."

Upon hearing such a thing, Giselda's hands twisted together like two ivory serpents, and her eyes became gushing fountains of bitter tears.

"Woe is me, sad and miserable creature," she moaned: "trying to save my beloved, I have brought him to his end; trying to end my sorrow, I have made it eternal!"

The messenger, standing erect at the door, murmured feebly: "My dear lady, remember that the Viceroy awaits your response."

Said the lady: "Go forth, hurry, faithful servant, and tell the cruel Viceroy to have mercy on poor Giselda's fate; remind him that a noble lady placed her faith in his good intentions and in his word, and it is beneath a gentleman to fail to measure up. Tell him that my husband is brave and strong and will serve him with his life if he softens his torments . . . Go, hurry, my friend; kneel at the feet of this evil man and soften his heart of bronze with your pleadings, for God and your lord will be pleased."

The messenger left again, and again returned, with two rivers of tears like crystal threads along the furrows of his face. He stopped in front of the lady without daring to say a word.

"Speak!" she exclaimed, with great turmoil in her heart.

"Oh, my poor lady! The evil one told me that for once and for all, you are to appoint the room facing the plaza, to the east, for he wishes to see your face with the first ray of the sun . . . and that as soon as the room is prepared, you are to send me to advise him . . . and that has to be within a quarter of an hour, oh my most mournful lady, unless you want to see your noble husband, my lord, dragged through the streets of the village."

Giselda raised her eyes upwards, full of tears like two goblets brimming with bile: "There is no salvation for me! O merciless fate, you have finally conquered a noble and chaste wife! Dear and noble husband! Today's perverse destiny decrees that Giselda render her honor for your life, but tomorrow your wife will turn over her life for your honor!"

The high and powerful Viceroy of those lands went to sleep with Giselda accompanied by the sound of drums and his armed troops, for he wanted the shame and insult to be public and well known.

When the lady saw him approach in such a manner, she hid her face in her hands and groaned frenetically:

"O God Almighty! Send fire from heaven upon this monster before he crosses my threshold, for he carries on his breath great offense to my lineage, and I am just a miserable and feeble female . . . How do you expect me, Our Lord, to resist such shame until tomorrow?"

The high and powerful Viceroy entered her chamber as the lady exclaimed those words. His face was resplendent, burning like coals, and his fat fingers were laden with golden rings studded with fine jewels. Lady Giselda was as white as a lily in the moonlight, and her unadorned hands were draped alongside her mourning clothes like two fallen lilies.

The room facing the plaza was adorned like a wedding chamber, but the awaited wedding was of outrage rather than pleasure.

The Viceroy took the lady's hand and led her to the alcove.

While he removed his jacket, she heaved a great sigh.

"What makes you sigh so, my lady?" the Viceroy asked.

"I sigh for my husband."

"Sigh no more, my lady, for the Viceroy swears to you on his crown that tomorrow at daybreak you will see the mirror of your eyes, the flower of your lips."

And the Viceroy laughed like a wolf going for the kill.

The powerful Viceroy jumped atop the bed, and it creaked with rage; when the lady entered, the chaste spouse, it became mute with fright.

The Viceroy is fast asleep, and his snores can be heard from the plaza; the lady sleeps not, for offense does not lead to slumber as does pleasure; the lady begs God's forgiveness for her sins, since her life is over.

All through the streets of the village, soldiers drunk with wine from hurled wineskins run about with torches lit, disturbing the quiet with their shrieking and barking like strange dogs. All around the house they sing and laugh like evil spirits. The lady sinks her face into the pillow to keep from hearing them, soaking it with her tears.

The night of mourning is long, interminable, like a night of hell.

The Viceroy is fast asleep; the lady awake, weeping, and at the first light of dawn, she jumps up from bed.

As she fastens her jacket she hears great noises . . . the squealing of trumpets, beating of drums, stomping and neighing of horses. She stiffens with dismay, thinking they are bringing her freed husband forth.

The Viceroy awakens and smiles with satisfaction.

"Would you like, noble lady, to see what is going on?"

Lady Giselda approaches the window, burning with shame.

The plaza is surrounded by armed men bearing helmets that sparkle in the rays of the rising sun, with their hands firmly on their harquebuses. Right in the middle a very long pole rises up . . . from the pole hangs a cord, and from the cord, a body swings back and forth, like ripe fruit ready to fall to the ground . . . Lady Giselda sees it, lets out the most terrible of howls, and falls to the ground.

The most high and powerful Viceroy of those lands leaves satisfied with the rebellious village, surrounded by his men-at-arms.

At the village gate, he stops his warhorse—white as a drop of milk and haughty as a damsel—and he tosses the keys to houses and prisons on the ground, ordering his heralds to issue forth a call. Sounding trumpets and waving flags, the heralds announce that the very high and powerful Viceroy of those lands has done justice in the name of the King.

No living soul listens to that announcement in the deserted village, which seems a cemetery. The only audience is a head with closed eyes, a long white beard imbedded above the door with a nail, crying tears of blood that fall upon the silk, jeweled tunic of the powerful Viceroy.

As the troops depart, an immense black cloud can be seen in the distance to the west, advancing toward the village. It is a great flock of crows.

Who is the courteous gentleman with soft eyes, soaked in sadness, whose body is graceful as a reed and who goes about like a suffering soul with no other company than that of an old page who follows on his heels, shuffling like a ghost? It is a noble foreigner from faraway lands who has come to serve the King, without understanding the language of the palace; for that reason he mixes with no one and joins neither festivities nor soirees. The young men look upon him with envy, the tender ladies with love, for he is handsome as the midday sun and young as a page of the Queen Mother. But he is indifferent to all and keeps apart, his thin body waving like a reed and his dark eyes soaked in sadness, as if he had left heart and thoughts back in those faraway lands whence he came.

Great bonfires light up the palace. The King is taking a wife for the third time, and the realm rejoices for the third time in celebration of the King's wedding. The King takes a bride and the people celebrate, once again, the good fortune of the King.

All the grandees go to court to congratulate the King and ask him for favors, for, whenever the King marries, he gives them out generously, as if he wants his royal joy to reach everyone in the kingdom.

The very high and powerful Viceroy of those lands is present as well. He has come to the palace to request something. He is a count, a marquis, a duke . . . he wishes to be a prince, for all that he has seems little to him.

The King listens to him and smiles, granting him what he wants.

The new prince goes down the stairs of the palace drunk with pride, his face resplendent, shining like burning coals, with his fat fingers covered with rings of gold embedded with fine jewels.

From the other direction, the young gentleman from faraway approaches with his page behind him, quiet and rigid like a ghost. The gentleman's body waves like a reed; his eyes are as dark as pain as he slowly draws near, dragging his scarlet cape behind him like a train of blood.

At the first landing, the noble and the Viceroy stand face-to-face.

The Viceroy says to him scornfully: "Get out of the way, beardless whippersnapper, for a prince is passing."

The gentleman stops, and, suddenly understanding the language of the palace, exclaims mockingly:

"Health to the new prince!" He raises his right arm as fast as lightning and buries the chiseled dagger into the prince's chest.

"Mercy!" cries the prince, jolting like a tree being cut down.

"The same mercy you had on me, foul assassin," responds the stranger with flames in his eyes, and he stuck the steel into the prince one more time.

"Oh, Giselda! . . . Forgive me!" murmurs the prince, recognizing her as he falls to the ground.

But with clenched teeth, she answers immediately: "Let Him forgive you, if He so wills, if the contrition is authentic!"

With the third stroke, his body divides in two and the powerful Viceroy of those lands gives his soul up to God.

The foreigner quickly leaves the palace, body waving like a reed in a storm, eyes full of darkness. The scarlet cape follows, hanging from the left arm, dragging on the ground like a train of blood.

The old page follows, stiff and silent, like a ghost, with a lively smile, full of joy.

THE ROSE-COLORED SECRET

The doctor was mulling over the presentation he had promised to deliver in Vienna at the Physiology Conference as he went up the stairs. He mentally clarified some of the more complex aspects; he went back to the original hypotheses; he perfected and reframed the form it would take, from beginning to end, with the secret delight of an author proud of his work, like a father at the delivery of a sound, healthy son.

So distracted was he in his musings that he forgot to greet the doorman with his usual good humor; he didn't even notice the polite respect with which the man got up, paying no attention to the muddy footstep the doctor left on the marble stairway. Nor did he see the powdery mark left on his jacket as he passed by the boy with the bread basket when they crossed paths.

Click, clack, click! his soles clattered up the white stairs with the hurried habit of a busy man who for years has been counting his hours carefully. He climbed without even realizing it until, when he got to the landing, he saw a clerk from one of the boutiques leaving with a large cardboard box. Then, gesturing to the chambermaid not to close the door, he paused a moment to let the clerk by, and with a friendly bow of his head he entered, to the surprise of the maid. He went straight to the patient's room with the confidence of habit, without bothering to have himself announced.

Everything was dark and still, more so than usual, and his steps seemed to soften too, as if the rug had grown thicker since the day before, but the doctor was familiar enough with the place to go ahead with his eyes closed. He quickly crossed the room without brushing against furniture and turned left, toward the chamber door. He was surprised to see the door barely ajar, and, beyond, quiet seemed to reign as well. What was going on? Had that poor sufferer who never seemed able to rest finally drifted off to sleep? He hoped so, as he cautiously pushed open the door. It gave way, silently sliding over the rug, leaving a wide, empty space before the doctor's eyes. He raised his head, and at that very moment his sight was wounded by a dazzling glare that seemed from a dream: a sudden, sharp vision hit him like an unexpected shot. There in front of him, instead of the old furniture covered with jars and medicine bottles, against the opposite wall between two balconies covered with curtains and cloths, was a lovely, lavish Louis XV armoire, whose magnificent mirror served as a frame for the most beautiful, bold vision of a Van Beers painting. It was a female figure, very blond and very white with a great sweep of hair on her head and her feet in dainty, toylike shoes. Between head and foot was a swan's neck and a young Diana's bust. In the role of great lady, she wore a tunic of the finest white lace, held by a rose tie on each shoulder; two divinely shaped arms held toward her back; long stockings of black silk molded the curve of two perfect legs. In short, it was a gentle lady in the intimacy of her toilette, which could have been titled "Trying on the Corset."

Recovered from his first surprise, the doctor realized his situation and error, his eyes still wounded by the Van Beers. Still, he remained immobile for a moment, looking at the lovely maiden with the slightly twisted neck, folded hands holding a bouquet of ribbons next to her body, gaze fixed on the mirrored corset. Her expression was abstract, as if she were also mulling over some thought, with her eyes half closed. Suddenly, oh tricks of fate, her gaze met with two carbuncles shining in the shadow. The effect was extraordinary and instantaneous: an expression of intense dismay froze the lady, taking all the color from her face. The doctor felt he had been caught, and he didn't know whether to flee like the perpetrator of some evildoing, or to remain awkward and indelicate by the door. A gallant look of confusion covered his face as if to ask forgiveness. The lady dared to turn her head a bit; on her snowy face was a reddish tinge, a sudden carmine, livelier than the ties at her shoulders, as if the tones of her lips had spread out over the silken skin. Modesty, of course! She had just recognized the intruder. She verified that recognition in an instant. Was it real or imaginary that the startled look melted away into a kind of mental smile of indefinite gesture? The doctor took advantage of that moment of doubt. His whole expression turned into a hymn of mute, fervent approval, in delicate homage from a fine connoisseur; he doubled over in a profound bow and the door closed slowly, like the curtain of a theater, on the Van Beers fantasy. But the luminous vision remained before him through the room, the hallway, the vestibule.

The chambermaid rushed over when she heard the door open again, and was more amazed by the quick exit than she had been at the unexpected entrance. On the other hand, the chronically sick patient on the second floor found the doctor even better-humored and expansive than usual.

The lady and the doctor are well known in social circles. More than once they have met at theaters or performances, and when they exchange glances, a mysterious current holds their gaze. The carmine of her lips spreads over her face, and a recondite tribute of admiration colors his eyes. The bittersweet memory has a trace of spicy flavor for them both, the tempting suggestion of forbidden fruit, and they both savor the feeling for a moment of naughty delight. Van Beers has tilted toward the eighteenth century. Then it vanishes, and that instant of mute intelligence remains unknown to all, a secret, a little rose-colored secret. Reddish like those cheeks, like those ties at the shoulder, the sweet little secret of a gentleman doctor and a lovely lady of Van Beers.

THE PITCHFORK PRONG

When she'd finished taking her baking out of the oven, Pubilla[3] had her breakfast of mint soup and garlic toast and got dressed to get an early start to Suriola. She combed her hair and straightened up, taking the long, fresh-smelling grain napkin to wrap up her pastry. Whenever she baked, she made an extra piece the length of her hand. They said she was very good at making pastry, and it was the favorite sweet around the house. She always took pride in that, but today even more, because the treat was for her aunt in Suriola, the one she loved so much, who had raised her when she lost her mother at the age of four. And this pastry had turned out perfect; blond like strands of gold, neither too thick nor too thin, fleshy and fluffy (her uncles

---

[3] Pubilla, literally translated as "heiress," refers to an oldest daughter who will inherit the family's land. Since *heiress* does not convey the meaning of Pubilla in a rural setting and since no proper names appear in this story, I have personalized the protagonist by using her title as a name.

had bad teeth and weren't up for chewing crusty things). It was topped off with bits of melted sugar and pine nuts, garnished with anchovies and candied quince. If it weren't for that little burned spot on the lower edge, it was a professional job. She couldn't bear the imperfection, so she moistened her finger with a little brandy, anointed the spot, and sprinkled flour on it. She looked at it with satisfaction, maybe even a little vanity, before she carefully covered it up with the nice, clean cloth.

It was six-thirty by the time she unbarred the little door to take the shortcut. When she said good-bye to her father, he came out of the stable and asked her: "Did you remember the prong?"

"I put it in the basket last night."

He was referring to the one that got broken, he didn't know exactly how, by the clumsy helper the last day of gathering alfalfa: "If he can't fix it, bring it back, and I'll use it to clear out the water pipes."

"Very well, Father . . . and good day to everyone."

"Good-bye, dear, and give my best to Auntie and the uncles."

Carrying a large basket and a shawl folded over her arm, she left amidst the tumult of excited dogs barking infernally.

Dawn had just broken, and the earth was covered by dull, gray tones of a metal goblet. The morning breeze touched her skin softly, like tiny fingernails of a babe, and the ground was slippery with frost.

She passed the manure heap, which was steaming like a stove and perfuming the air with its warm breath, so smelly it burned her eyes.

Pubilla quickly went down the orchard steps. The cabbage up above and the herbs around the edges looked whitish, as if she had sprinkled sugar on them too, and, below, a few scratchy signs showed that the rabbits had nibbled on the chickpeas. From the oak grove issued a great chirping of birds.

Before she entered the dim light of the forest, the girl looked all around, just as one who reviews a lesson learned long ago, and her heart trembled, agitated by a regaining of peaceful fortune. If she dared, she would have frolicked like the dogs do every day, making a big commotion simply because a new day has arrived. In the twenty-four hours that each one offers, changes are fast if the repertoire is to be complete.

So when she got out of the forest to take the main road, the world no longer seemed like a dullish metal goblet. Still moist, the air was now clear, filled with iridescent transparencies, like a glass freshly rinsed.

She had always heard people complain about that stretch of road that went on and on, but she loved it. As she walked along with her little partridge steps, she enjoyed letting herself go, distracted, taking in all the fleeting impressions that came to mind, just as the merry passersby did, without having to watch every step for hollows and bumps that might make one stumble, or for the claws of hawthorns and brambles that grabbed at her skirt along the little paths with the tenacity of beggars. And what a view she had from one end of the plain to the other! Farmhouses, hamlets, stream beds, groves, breaks, ponds, hermitages, stepping stones, slopes, stone mounds, turns, meadows, outcrops, sandy spots, little bridges, channels . . . just like a Nativity scene, also peppered with flocks of sheep, peasants, toilers of the land, oxcarts, caravans of wanderers, honeysuckle, rosemary, the sounds of horses and chickens, the cracking of whips, tumbling water, goldfinches wagging their tails, magpies in flight, bluish smoke in the distance, bells ringing, lizards scurrying about, a hunter's shots and the yelping of greyhounds . . . who could keep track of so many sensations of every kind!

The sun was now behind the crest line, blushing as if it had just done some mischief, reflecting its rays in the windows of Nespleda, and the top of the farmhouse at the summit was still clothed in darkness, like a bus with its lights on. A little further on, Curriol Castle in the distance, surging out of the plain and hiding the foothills, seemed suspended between earth and sky.

She ran across women cleaning the base of the grape plants at Gambí, all in a row with their little rakes at their shoulders.

"Where are you off to, Pubilla, to Suriola?"

"Yes, that's right, if you'd like to come along . . ."

"I hear your aunt still isn't quite well?"

"They had to take off excess water."

"Bad news, at her age. Water in the pipe, meat in the tummy, that's what's best."

"You're right about that!"

"It's the best remedy, that's what they say."

"May God grant it."

"Good-bye, dear."

"Farewell, ladies."

She hears them chatting and laughing for a few more minutes, then she is once again alone on the long road, and her eyes and heart go back to her beloved countryside.

What was that blurry white she saw, like dust, to the right at the end of the fields? Of course, she was already approaching Mata-rodona, her uncle's town. That's it! Now she could make out the shape of the bell tower, like a cone for candy put upside-down. The place still took her by surprise! Probably because that village looked so different with each change in the light. At this hour, it seemed made of milk, and yet she knew that the houses weren't whitewashed; they were all the color of home-made bread.

She scratched her right cheek where the sun was hitting her, making the skin itch like a burr. Between the warmth of the sun and her walking, her blood tickled all over, and the more she moved, the more she wanted to move; her legs went on their own without her even feeling them, and the road seemed to melt beneath her feet. She had already passed Birell, all sunken alongside the road, with its sprinkling of haystacks and snowfall of geese honking scandalously. She crossed the ford in the stream, where she used to stop and rest on her way to Suriola when she was little, making the trip twice a week to learn how to read from the local teacher. She could now see Puntís, the old fortified farmhouse, attacked during the last Carlist War and falling apart stone by stone in solitude, like a pomegranate ready to crumble.

Near the earth-colored tower, a fellow was preparing his nine o'clock snack on a little cane fire. The wind brought forth smoke and the odor of frying beyond the crops, and the sun sparkled on the metallic cap of the official.

"Good morning, sir."

"Good morning to you, young lady. Want some breakfast?"

"No, may you enjoy it."

Now the land was neither metal goblet nor rinsed glass but a golden cup, shining and reflecting warmth. The space twinkled with each of her heartbeats, splashing streaks of broom as if to make the Corpus holiday come early. Yellowish hues of squash, orange, sulfur, all mixed together, covered the scars of stripped areas and bathed the nearby fields. In the middle of them, as if drawn by lazy vacationers, the mother-of-pearl road slipped along toward the light amethyst of the mountains, which covered the horizon, spotted with dark shadows of birds in flight.

As Suriola came into view in the distance, like a handful of wheat nestled into the plain covered with tender greens like a long brush stroke, Pubilla came across another passerby. He was a wanderer, shabby and dirty, with a full wineskin hanging from his shoulder. He was preceded and announced from quite a distance by the stinging odor of dark wine, stale tobacco, and filth, which bothered the young woman's nose much more than the dung heap she had passed earlier when she left her Rambla farmhouse.

"Hello, Roget . . ."

"Hu . . . ,"[4] the man growled as a response, looking aslant at her without raising his eyelids.

---

[4] The same monosyllable characterizes Ànima, who represents the forces of evil in Albert's *Solitude.*

Pubilla knew him well enough from handing out bread to him more than once at the farmhouse. He was from a Mata-rodona family and they were good people, but he was lazy and fond of the tavern; he had left his home while still young to dedicate himself to a lower sort of life. His family wanted nothing to do with him.

What friendly greetings she received as she went up the hill toward town—from men and women, and one might say even from the animals! And what joy her arrival brought to her aunt, with her visit and the tasty gift. Auntie was delighted, asking one question after another without giving the girl time to reply; she wanted to show her all the new acquisitions at once: the baby ducks and the drakes, the two carnation blossoms Pubilla had tended herself on her last visit—prettier than the dahlias; the new felt cushion; slippers the doctor had brought so her feet wouldn't get cold . . .

The aunt heaved her heavy, dropsical belly to and fro with difficulty, but she wouldn't stop until Pubilla, laughing and grabbing her by the shoulders, pushed her onto a bench by force, ignoring the old lady's protests.

"What luck that you came today, sweetie . . . the very day your uncle went to the fair and I would have been alone all day."

"Oh, really? Alone, huh? We'll see what kind of a feast we'll have, just you and me, to punish him for taking off when he knew I was coming!"

Pubilla ordered her aunt to stay put, for today she wouldn't let her do a thing. Today would be as if her aunt had hired a maid, and the young woman rolled up her sleeves and reached for the broom. From bedrooms to cellar, from pantry to entry, she cleaned up everything and imposed order in that house, somewhat neglected because of the lady's illness. She straightened out the chicken coop and brought in enough water for a few days, while the stew was boiling in the hanging pot. Then she made an omelet of the eggs and sausage she'd brought from her farm at Rambla, and they sat down to eat. The aunt, overcome with gratefulness, shed a few tears, enchanted with that niece she had raised, who was worth more than her weight in gold. After the meal, the young woman washed the dishes, letting her aunt dry the spoons. She set the supper, already prepared, on the stove to keep warm and went out on the porch to do some sewing. Chatting all the while, she went over all the clothing in the house, putting a hem in a skirt and mending here and there; then she took her ailing aunt by the arm to help her walk, and they went out to the orchard. When her uncle arrived, it was after four, and they realized the whole day had gone by. She still hadn't gone to the shop to see about the prong.

She said good-bye to aunt and uncle, and hurried off to the smith shop.

"That's not something I can fix, Pubilla . . . If you like, next time I go to Figueres, I'll see about it."

"I'll tell my father . . . Good-bye, smithy, until next time."

"You're going back to Rambla now? It's getting late."

"Well, I'll hurry. When the stable is waiting, even the lame horse looks good."

"You always look good, Pubilla."

"Good thing your wife didn't hear that, she'd have a scowl for me."

And with a smile she took her leave, heading down the hill and looking very good indeed, if not for the awaiting stable, because of the strength of her twenty years.

"The smithy was right, though, it's quite late, and I must get going."

The metal goblet, the rinsed glass, the golden cup had all transformed into a bowl of polished copper. Everything glistened in a fantasy of polychrome, warm colors of a fall symphony, linings of fire highlighted the profile of blue mountains and clusters of dark-green trees. A band of swifts formed ink spots across the sky as they whistled at the steeple brightened like burning coal. Cows on their way home from the trough drooled as they watched the long shadows moving across the earth. The hollow of the sky deepened with dense shades of violet porcelain and golden sparkles. The highway disappeared into the distance like a strip of white linen, and the last dawdling flocks of sheep returned with their fleece tinted in rosy tones . . . it was a marvel.

On the first stretch of road, Pubilla crossed paths with a number of people she knew, returning from their day's work; then gradually men and beasts became sparse as outlines grew deeper. The blocks of the bridge didn't seem their own size; they looked like soldiers on watch; a little hill became an imposing mountain; the stream turned into a raging torrent.

A little beyond Puntís, a bright spot appeared in the sky, the Shepherd's Star.

She hurried on, getting a little worried about the impending twilight. Her father didn't like her crossing the forest after dark, and she didn't want to get reprimanded.

An owl hooted, and the unexpected companion comforted her. As she passed Birell, she was glad to hear an invisible dog barking at her furiously from some nearby patio, as if her scent were that of an enemy.

A burst of intense light behind Curriol Castle; a flash of clarity across the sky; brushstrokes of blood red on one peak and another crest, and the sun set suddenly, in the blink of an eye. A fine ashen dust chilled everything, sky and earth. The distances melted away like warm breath on glass, and there was a moment of complete silence, as if the world withdrew into itself before the arrival of the deepest mysteries.

As darkness fell, she still had a third of the way to go, and she stepped up her pace even more, though yesterday's baking and today's cleaning and walking made her aware of her tiredness.

Ten minutes later a marvelous new transformation occurred. The ashes were whisked away by an unseen fan; a rather impenetrable, deceiving limpidity faded the lines of landscape and farmhouses, making the surroundings phantasmagoric.

Suddenly, a few stars shone high up, a toad croaked, a frog bellowed, a screeching sounded in the uncertain distance, and two silent crows traced lines across the sky, one after the other, leaving a streak of black against the melting celestial opal. From inside a window, or perhaps on a ledge up the mountainside, a little light sparkled and then flickered out.

Like a virginal smile against her skin, a fine, penetrating, cold breeze passed by on its way to the infinite.

The world was now a pale silver chalice, over which the white host of a moon was suspended like an immense pearl. At that moment, she entered the forest. Ten minutes more and the dogs of the Rambla would announce her arrival to her father. But . . . what was that odor, like rotting carrion, that suddenly accosted her nose?

Before she can react, a cluster of bushes moves and the beast is upon her. Fright keeps her from yelling out. It was he, no doubt about it; she can't see him, but the odor is much stronger now than it was this morning: the bitter breath of dark wine, stale tobacco, and filth. Burning into her brain, certain memories flashed by like electric sparks: that poor maid who swore she was innocent, that she had no boyfriend, that some unknown being had jumped her from out of the bushes; a much more painful memory, of her mother who died so young, inflicted with a mysterious illness, inexplicable to everyone at the farm, but revealed on her deathbed to the aunt from Suriola.

Those memories gave her a terrible energy to flee from the danger, but before she had a chance, an iron hand fell upon her, turned her on her back, and struggled to subject her arms and cover her mouth. She got herself up like a serpent hit by a scythe, grappling ferociously, and, embraced, they tumbled down, turning over and over. Pubilla senses that the man is not strong, and with a supreme effort she can save herself. Between bites and shrieks, she kicks furiously. When she least expects it, she hears a muffled howl and the iron arms encircling her ribs begin to give way. With a violent push, she manages to turn him over, and now she is on top of the monster. She's got him! Instinct guides her like a blind man's aid. She's aware for a second of how awful her own face must look. When she finds him disabled, overcome between her legs, she jumps up. She still has the wherewithal to gather the basket and smooth her hair.

She can't imagine how she made those last few hundred meters on foot, but she realizes it's not as late as she thought, for they're waiting for her to come to supper, all together in the kitchen.

"Oh, no," she says. "I ate late with Auntie: to give them some company, you know? And since I did all the cleaning and straightening there, I'm exhausted. I'll just go to bed, if you don't mind."

She spoke from the shadows without showing her face; they all attributed her weary voice to the tiredness of her day's work.

"Go ahead, dear, go on. You always do too much when you go to Suriola. I'm going to tell your aunt not to let you," her father said kindly.

"Wait, I'll put on the light," offered the elderly maid.

"I have matches and the candle on the nightstand. Good night."

And without waiting for anyone to say more, she went up the stairs in the dark.

A day went by, and another, a week, and several more days passed.

Pubilla is a little pale, like a rose too long in the pitcher, and she complains of headaches, but other than that, nothing betrays anything out of the ordinary or suggests her ordeal.

A little over a month later, the oxherd from Mitjà farm, who has placed traps to catch rabbits, goes to have a look, and crouched in his hiding place, a smell reaches his nostrils from time to time, so foul it makes him dizzy. As he approaches the opening of the Rambla, the odor becomes stronger. The hole leads to a cave among the rocks to the west, only three hundred meters from the farmhouse but on the other side of the slope. The oxherd sticks his head inside and sees a man completely stretched out. The man is dead, and for some time now. As if pursued, scared, the "father" of the oxen runs to the Rambla farmhouse and shouts out the news; he does the same at his own farmhouse, the Mitjà; he passes by the Rellissos, what does he have a tongue for? Within a quarter of an hour, the news has spread like dust, and people come from all around. The judge arrives from Suriola and the doctor from Molleda at the proper time.

Roget lies sideways at the entrance of the cave on an uneven, graded landing. His head hangs down from the edge so that it is lower than the rest of his body. His mouth is open, his upturned lip betrays a violent spasm that death has frozen on his face. His reddish beard and head, like stubbles of a dry brush, are as long as two fingers, and in his nostrils and one eye, rolled back, black flies with metallic sparkles are embedded like ticks.

Pubilla's father has lent a hand barrow to transport the body, and in spite of the stench, he and many others join the retinue to the Molleda cemetery to watch the undressing and rudimentary autopsy.

After a brief examination, the doctor declares what Roget died of. A purplish spot in the fat on his left side indicates a puncture wound that, not healed, led to peritonitis. Hunger and thirst did the rest.

As the investigation begins, many recall that a month or so ago, Roget went through their towns with a group of vagabonds. Near Birell there was a fight about who knows what, and after that Roget was seen wandering on those roads alone. It seemed logical to attribute the crime to the former companions, and orders were issued to arrest them wherever they were found. But God only knows where they had scattered to by then; Roget's demise wasn't a great loss to anyone; his relatives didn't want to take part in any inquiry; so the judge shrugged his shoulders and ordered the dead man to be buried.

Pubilla's father returned home with his head down. He saw her seated on the stairway to the lower orchard; he drew near and sat down beside her. She noticed his pale and drawn face, as if he hadn't slept all night.

"Aren't you well, Father?"

"Listen, dear, what did you do with the prong?"

The blood left her veins.

"Don't be afraid, and tell me the truth."

"I buried it in the terrace of the forest."

"Good and buried?"

"Yes, Father."

"You're sure no one will find it?"

"Yes, father."

"All right, then. Tonight I'll take the rest of the pitch-fork apart and get rid of it as soon as I can."

The poor man did not dare to ask anything further.

Our lives tie us to certain fates, that is, to a series of de-termined fatalities.

Pubilla has daughters, fresh and pretty as flower buds, and they go to Suriola to learn to read and sew. Every time they go, their mother feels a smothered heartbeat, and she doesn't breathe easily until they are again by her side. But the Rambla is her place, she bears three hundred years of ancestors rooted in that clod of land, and the farmhouse is the apple of everyone's eye, the future of those here now and those to come. Even the forest seems sacred, and they wouldn't cut down as much as a single oak tree from it.

No doubt one day her daughters will suffer the same terror she did, just as her mother and her grandmother did, perhaps . . . But, who can help it? Fate is inexorable.

KNEADINGS OF A DAUGHTER-IN-LAW

The leavening piece, puffy, softly stiff, had the form and swelling of a woman's breast. Caressing it brought an agreeable sensation to Beleta as she made it jump back and forth between her hands. Kneading was a truly pleasurable job; she had never tired of it no matter how many loaves she had to make or how hard it was to get the dough to rise. She sprinkled flour in the trough and formed the crown of the loaf in the middle. Whenever she saw or touched flour, or even smelled that odor like no other, she thought of her mother-in-law, may God be with her. When it was her mother-in-law who did the kneading and headed the household, whenever she sifted flour, she would repeat the lines that went: "Godmother, Godmother, while you sift flour, let me out of the sack, *catric, catrac.*" She never went further than those opening words of the tale. Beleta would have liked to know the rest of the story—Why did they put the girl in a sack?—but she never had the nerve to ask her mother-in-law to tell her the rest . . . It seemed so childish to tell tales! If her sisters-in-law had been little, or if she had had children herself . . . She was a good woman, her mother-in-law; even now, when Beleta thought of her, tears came to her eyes and she got a lump in her throat. She had suffered so much, spiritually, in that house! Her father-in-law was so stubborn, and so stingy! Good lord! What good had it done him to save every penny? He had to leave it all here anyway, didn't he? Other people benefited from it, though . . .

Beleta pressed vigorously over and over again into the leavening with her fist; she folded the dough over, thickening the circle as her train of thought continued. Good heavens! She could still see him as on that blustery morning, when she inadvertently discovered his big secret. The kneading room was so dark in the early morning, you nearly had to grope your way along. Only around the window did a little light come in, making a diffuse circle of misty blue, but all the rest seemed full of a dense smoke that hid everything. It was so dark and smoky in the corners, you could almost slice it. For that very reason . . .

Beleta thought: "I always tried to get the bread a bit bland; let's see if I can get it right this time" . . . and she added a little salt to the water in the bucket, sprinkled a little more flour on the yeast, rubbed her hands with another dusting, and returned again and again to kneading and pounding the dough. The constant *catric, catrac* in her mind from her mother-in-law's tale helped her with the rhythmic task. In the bit of yard between the oven and the sacking area, it was so dark, the air was so still and steady, that she and her mother-in-law had decided it would be a good place to put the new hen, with two dozen well-chosen eggs, plump as waxed apples. Of course that was a lot of eggs, but the hen was so proud, and she covered them well with her wings all puffed out; still, one couldn't count on it. So just in case, she had added some old rags to cover up the basket. Just as she was doing that, her father-in-law came into the kneading room and, without noticing her presence, went straight to the back, where a pile of small baskets for distributing coal was waiting to be taken to the surrounding towns next week.

The room had been divided into two, years ago: one side had a floor of old tiles, thick and rustic like bricks from an oven; the other had been roughly pebbled with stones from the riverbed. When they removed the partition, the floor was left as it was. The coal baskets, stacked up in threes, occupied the lower part of the pebbled section. Her father-in-law had gone straight for the right corner, where there was a bit of dim light from the window. He took out a coal basket from the third row of the pile, another from the second, still another from the third, which was on the ground. Behind it was a sort of cave, a dark hiding place. The man squatted down and began to scrape right into the corner formed by the two walls. Beleta's eyes, adjusted to the darkness, could see his movements well enough, but she couldn't tell what he was doing, crouched there, scraping quietly, she didn't know at what. She fixed her gaze, but still couldn't tell.

Her heart froze, as if something terrible was about to befall her. She would have fled from the spot if she could; she feared that her father-in-law would think she was spying on him. She hadn't left right at the beginning, since she didn't know he had any secret business there, and now it was too late; she felt as if her feet were stuck to the ground between the winch and the sacks of strips. Meantime, crouched over and immobile, he kept on poking silently into that corner, the farthest from the entry to the room. Suddenly, Beleta heard a strange ping, a small, sharp sound, as if metal had hit one of the pebbles of the floor. He must have some kind of tool in his hands, no doubt. She hadn't noticed that he was carrying anything when he came in . . . five minutes passed, maybe ten, how many? She couldn't even guess how much time was slipping by between her father-in-law's mysterious job and her fearful observance of it . . . She was in a kind of trance . . . Other odd noises, almost inaudible, reached her from the dark cave in the corner. Finally, he struggled to get up, cursing; he straightened himself on legs that were asleep from being in that odd position; he stomped to waken them, pulled his pants above his waist, shook the dust off his knees with a few gruff strokes, and tightened his belt. Now Beleta could see exactly what he was doing. He paused for a moment, then began to cover up the hole he had just opened, arranging the baskets in their rows, back in their original position. If Beleta hadn't been there, no one could have imagined the strange maneuver that had just taken place. He slowly passed right in front of her, toward the entry. Now she could see the iron digging tool he had, the little hand rake the women used to gather grass to feed the rabbits. She had used it herself many times.

When she could no longer hear his footsteps and was sure he was gone, she left as well and ran up the stairs to her bedroom. As she passed in front of the little mirror beside the window, she glanced at herself and saw the face of a dead person, white as wax, and she realized what a fright she had suffered. For days and days, she couldn't get her father-in-law out of her head. What on earth could it be that he had hidden in the kneading room? For it surely must be something he loved dearly, something he didn't want anyone to know about. Beleta thought about it day and night; she ruminated and puzzled, without getting any answer to her mental question. Until, one afternoon, mother- and sister-in-law were out at the orchard, where there was a lot of work to catch up with after a long stretch of bad weather. The men—her husband and his father—hadn't yet come back from the mountain, where they were looking for coal. She was alone in the house. She took the basket of clothes to wash, locked the outer door, stuck her hand in through the cat hole, and hung the key on the little hook inside. The next-door neighbor was sewing outdoors, and Beleta said to her, "If anyone comes, please tell them that I went down to the river." She started down the road, but not to the river. She turned around and went back to the house, going in through the back door, which she had left unlocked on purpose. She had already washed the few items she had in the basket in the sink half an hour ago. When she crossed the threshold of the kneading room, her heart beat to *catric, catrac* of the old rhyme; she felt completely in suspense.

At this time of day, the room wasn't gloomy and shadowy as it was in the morning. The window faced west and was open from the floor to the panel of tile and lath. A broad, transparent swath entered on a slant like a dust of golden gauze, through which an infinity of wandering motes wafted back and forth, making it tremble like something alive. Hazy reflections sparkled on the walls, twinkling happily. The luminous sash brightened everything in the room, turning the mystery from terror into magic.

Beleta had no time to lose, so she quickly took the coal basket that was left in the first row out of the corner (the others in that row had been sold last week), and she fixed her avid, anxious stare on the stones. She was surprised that nothing seemed out of the ordinary. The pebbles of the floor were dirty and uneven, like some gaping old neglected thing, but they seemed uniform throughout the visible part. But her father-in-law had not moved from that spot, so whatever it was had to be right there. She kept looking, with all her senses on alert . . . "Surely I'm not mistaken?" The stone against the corner of the two walls might be a little bigger and shinier than the others, a little less dirty perhaps. The earth of the enclave was slightly less black and greasy, less compact, than the rest of the dirt. She would have to move that rock! That was the first thing to be done. She would not have known how to do that, but she remembered the slight, metallic ring and the digger in her father-in-law's hands. She ran to the entry to get the tool, and hunching down just as she had seen him do, she stuck a prong between wall and stone, and with soft firmness she wedged it in. It didn't take much, since the stone had been replaced recently; it gave way and came out quickly. Now she had it out of its nest, but her heart raced and a wave of panic overtook her. Inside, she could see nothing but dirt, damp dirt. "It can't be!" she said to herself. She had heard scratching, so she started to scratch too, goaded by anxiety. With her whole hand inside, she felt something hard. Finally! She set the dirt she was removing on one side and the other, very carefully uncovering the hidden object. What could it be? It was a thick covering of grainy iron, encrusted with dried mud and rust. It was flat on the ground, but upside down. She wasn't surprised at all when she picked it up and found the round opening of a jar. It was full of dirt, too. No, no, it wasn't dirt, it was something less compact, softer. Beleta grabbed a handful and held it under the streak of light that came down diagonally from the window. Good heavens! It was bran, rancid bran, old and discolored by time and burial. She spread her apron out on the floor and kept taking handfuls out, first what was surrounding the jar and then its contents. For the second time, she felt something hard at her fingertips. It was an old sock, all darned together; a man's sock, hand-knitted, of blue cotton, which had been dark blue when new, but many washings had made it sky-colored. It was stuffed, completely full, and it looked odd and deformed, like a sausage. It was very heavy indeed, for its size. Beleta untied it with great care, as if she were dealing with beehives, removing the black, twisted ribbon like a string. The old sock was nothing other than a pouch full of silver coins. Most of them must have been very old, for they were practically black; others were grayish, lead-colored (these looked familiar to her); still others had strange names that she had never seen or heard. She couldn't take the time to count, but to judge just by looking, she calculated that there must be several hundred duros, carefully piled in three columns, each one wrapped loosely in a sheet of brown paper, the three tied together with a black cord so they could stand straight in the sock. She returned them to their places exactly the way she found them, and she was about to put the strange purse back among the bran, when it occurred to her that the jar was very large for such a small parcel, and, moved by another sudden impulse, she stuck her hands back into the bran and scratched nervously. Her instinct hadn't deceived her. There was something else, hard as the sock she had just pulled out.

Controlling her impatience and putting all five senses to work, she emptied out all the bran, exposing some new mystery in the bottom of the jar. Even though at that moment the golden sash shone fully through the window, reverberating life throughout the kneading room, that spot was in the dark and her anxious desire still could not make out the contents. So, even though she hated to take the time in her hurried task, she went to the kitchen for matches and returned to her corner. She lit one up, putting her hand behind it to project the bit of light into the bottom of the jar, convinced she would find another sock. But no. Filling up the whole lower part of the jar, as if made to measure, covered up by a purple cloth, there was a basket made of palm leaves, old and moldy. An astonished Beleta discovered more coins inside the basket, not strange and ugly, but clean and shiny like little suns . . . gold pieces! How many were there? She didn't dare to take them out of their nest to count them, but then she didn't need to. Her mother-in-law had been from a well-off family, and when she married, her father had presented her with fifty pieces of gold—she said they were quarter doubloons—during the wedding banquet, given in, precisely, a palm-leaf basket. The happy bride had turned the basket over to the groom, and that was the last she saw of it. Beleta had heard her mother-in-law's story many times, always told in the same painful tone. There couldn't be the slightest doubt, then; the hidden treasure belonged to her mother-in-law. Beleta was terribly moved. If only she could tell her mother-in-law and share the joy of that find! But no, she had to reject that temptation, for the secret was not hers. It was her father-in-law's, and she had no right to tell anyone about it.

The light had faded suddenly; she had to hurry, or someone would discover her performing that clandestine task. Beleta rearranged things as best she could, filling the jar with bran and replacing the sky-blue sock. She covered the hiding place with muddy dirt, returned the stone to its position, put the basket back in the corner, and left the room.

For several days—she remembered it all as if it were today—she thought of nothing else. She hadn't been able to overcome her overwhelming curiosity, and perhaps she had done wrong to violate her father-in-law's secret. Yes, maybe she hadn't behaved properly, trying to pry into things she had no right to know, but it would be even worse to divulge the secret. If she did, everyone would be suspicious of her, especially her father-in-law, who was bad-tempered and resentful; he would never forgive her. Her spreading the secret around might even lead to some tragedy. For example, her husband, every bit as bad-tempered and money-grubbing as his father, might take it away with the excuse that someone might steal it; that after all he was to inherit everything in the end; by rights it belonged to him anyway.

Beleta's thoughts stopped suddenly, leaving her father-in-law behind and focusing on the job at hand. As she pounded the dough again and again in the trough, the bulk rose and softened. Beleta could hardly control it, and the sweat poured down her cheeks as if she were under a shower; it would have dripped onto the bread if she hadn't wiped it off with the insides of her elbows. Her chest was white with flour, her tangled, wispy hair, too, forming a blurry halo around her face. But gently pressing the delicate heaviness between her strong arms produced a warm, voluptuous emotion in the young woman, and she prolonged the task deliciously in spite of her weariness. Once she had the bread compact and round, she tore it up again by the handful, pulling at the ends to form misshapen strips, then billiard balls. Pressing them again with her fists, she pounded them against the wood once more and reincorporated them into the main mound. It was not until, exhausted but yearning, her kidneys gave the alert and she had to rest her aching back that her mind went back to her father-in-law and his antics. Yes, perhaps she had erred in spying, accidentally, on him, but after days and nights of wrestling with what to do, she ended up not saying anything to anyone, keeping that grand secret all to herself. She figured she would keep it forever, but as the saying goes, men propose but God disposes.

Because who could have suspected what would happen to her young sister-in-law? The older one was already married when Beleta came to live in that house, and the younger one was still a child. But the child was growing up, and before they realized it she was a woman. Everyone, including Beleta, found her lovely, and she was vigorous and clever as well. She was sweet-tempered and compassionate, like her mother; she never shirked hard work, and she would have taken food from her own mouth to give it to the first unfortunate person who passed by their door. Beleta loved her right from the start, and the two had always got along well, like two real sisters. That is why such a commotion sprang up when *that* happened. The kneading room was once again the setting, as it had always been, ever since she married into the household.

For several days, Beleta had noticed that the girl's face was always either completely red or completely white. "She must not be feeling well . . . Sometimes girls her age have such problems." After dinner on a very hot day, Beleta saw the girl pick up the jugs to go to the cold spring, a good way from town, and she took the jugs from her hands, saying, "If you don't mind, I'll go to the spring today . . . So many days inside the house, it would do me good to stretch my legs a little." The girl cheered up with that proposal, so while mother and daughter remained at the entry, Beleta went inside with jugs in hand, but once through the door she realized she had a stain on her apron from who knows what. Beleta was extremely neat and clean: "Good thing the other apron is nice and fresh." She set the jugs down by the door and went into the kneading room, where a basket held the smooth, folded laundry in that same *blessed*, dark corner by the winch. Just as she was tying her apron strings, her mother-in-law and sister-in-law came in. Their eyes hadn't made the adjustment to the darkness, so they didn't see her. She was about to speak when the girl burst into sobs and threw her arms around her mother's neck.

"It's true, mother, he's married . . . married, poor me!" she wept inconsolably.

The mother was horrified; she tried to calm herself down and, with a wisp of hope in her voice, asked: "How do you know he's married, sweetie?"

"He confessed it himself, Mother, when I told him we would have to get married."

"Have to get married?" Mother's eyes widened.

The girl's sobs shook her more violently than before: "Yes mother, I . . . I . . ."

Beleta had never seen such a terrified expression on her mother-in-law's face. Her legs started to give out as well, and she nearly collapsed to the floor.

"You mean you, my dearest? . . . What do you mean, for heaven's sake?"

For as many years as Beleta continued living in that house, she never forgot that scene between mother and daughter, the shameful confession, then the shock and desperation of the mother. When the wretched woman half recovered her senses, still trembling from the unexpected blow her daughter had just given her, she managed to say with a broken rasp that didn't seem her voice at all, "Let's go upstairs, my unlucky baby; someone could come in."

Stumbling and jerking as if she'd been beaten, she grabbed on to the railing, and the two, the mother with the help of her daughter, climbed the staircase.

As soon as the shuffle of footsteps faded, Beleta crept out on tiptoes with her heart oppressed as if by iron claws. She took hold of the jugs once again and went to the spring. Deeply moved, she ruminated as she walked along. "What a terrible blow for everyone, what a tragedy!" She saw it so clearly, like a flash of lightning, or as if she were reading it all in the pages of a book.

Her young sister-in-law had fine manners and was even a little fussy; she seemed more urban than rural. Since she was classy, she had tastes to match. Consequently, she didn't pay much attention to the peasant lads from around there who were eyeing her as a possible fiancée. On the other hand, as soon as she was approached by one of the newcomers that came to town with the army, she ignored her mother's advice and her brother's reproaches—for he couldn't see any good coming out of getting involved with an outsider who with his lousy salary would leave her hungry all her life—she started to go out with him. He was Castilian,[5] young and clever; his uniform was always nicely ironed and his hair neatened with brilliantine. Soon they were formally engaged. "And

---

[5] That is, he was not Catalan and therefore doubly an outsider.

now, all of a sudden," thought Beleta, "this awful tragedy, this frightful happening. Lucky my husband is still up in the mountains looking for coal!"

That evening the girl said she wasn't feeling well and went to bed early. At that point, the mother-in-law, all upset, her face covered with tears and pale as if recovering from a great illness, led Beleta into the kitchen.

"Bel . . . I love you as a daughter . . . and I want to tell you what's going on . . ."

"There's no need, my dear," she murmured, seating the older woman on a bench and pulling up a chair for herself, "I already know."

"You mean, it's already spread about?" She was horrified.

"No, don't worry about that. I was in the kneading room when you both came in this afternoon, and I heard what she told you, without meaning to."

The mother-in-law put her head in her hands. "What a terrible affront, Bel, what a thing to happen at the end of my days! And now, she can't even get married!" She paused to ask: "I don't know if you know . . ."

"Yes, yes, I heard everything," she said and, getting up her courage, added in an appeasing tone: "Although if you want to know what I think, maybe it's a blessing in disguise that she can't marry him. She's a good kid, and what can you expect from such a vile man?"

Her mother-in-law stared at her, appalled: "But what are we going to do, Bel, with my poor daughter? When your husband finds out, he'll kill her!"

Beleta softly put her hand on the old lady's trembling arm. "Don't despair, my dear. You know how the saying goes, 'God helps in time of great need,' and He'll help us get through this. Look, I've been mulling things over all afternoon, and if you like, I'll tell you what's been going through my head."

The woman's whole life was concentrated in her gaze at that moment: "Tell me, please, I don't see any solution, but . . ."

"As you know, my sister who lives up in the mountains wrote to me, saying she's practically paralyzed with pain. I was going to ask if I could go up to see her, and once I'm there, we could talk about this sad situation, and I wouldn't be surprised if she . . ."

Her mother-in-law's eyes turned into a fountain; her chin was jerking so violently that she couldn't get a word out.

And so in that corner of the kitchen next to the empty fireplace and beneath the pale light, the color of an egg yolk, reflecting off the brass lamp on the mantelpiece shelf, the two women, alone together, decided what could be done. When her husband returned with the fortnight's load, Beleta spoke to him of her wish to visit her sick sister. Off she went, carrying little household gifts from her mother-in-law for her sister, and when she came back a few days later, she lamented, exaggerating a bit, how weak her sister was, and that she really needed someone to help her for a while until she could recover her strength. She added, looking at her husband out of the corner of her eye:

"If only I could stay with her for a while . . . but I know I'm needed around here for the coal distribution, since I'm the one who handles it most . . ."

"No, of course you can't go," her husband replied naturally.

"That's what I told her," said Beleta, and added, slowly and diplomatically: "She said to me, 'If only your young sister-in-law could come up and run the household for a while, until I can take care of things myself, she'd be doing me a big favor'"—and, knowing how greedy her husband was, she calmly added—"'I'd pay her a decent salary, gratefully. Since there are three women in your house for now . . . with what you have to manage . . .'" Beleta stopped, but since no one said anything, she carefully said: "I told her I would talk to you, and since you're good people, willing to lend a hand whenever you can . . ."

The girl happily said yes right away, and her mother agreed as well. Beleta's husband gave in, thinking, "Maybe if she gets out of here for a while, she'll forget about that damned outsider," and that was the end of the conversation for the moment.

When mother- and daughter-in-law found themselves alone again (and at that point they sought each other out secretly whenever they could), the old woman exclaimed: "God will pay you, my dear. You were right. God sent you my way to take care of me." But then she added with a note of anxiety: "Except the part about a salary, we can't do it, and afterward, with whatever might be coming . . . How are we going to explain all that to your husband?"

Beleta smiled and said: "My dear, we don't need anything from anybody. You're richer than you think."

"Right, as rich as a cockroach, poor me!" She added plaintively: "If only your father-in-law hadn't wasted my dowry, which disappeared and I never saw it again."

"Don't worry, everything will work out, God willing."

Her husband went off to take care of the coal business, and Beleta asked her mother-in-law to get the girl out of the house for a good while under whatever pretext she could think of. When they were alone once again, Beleta repeated the activities of some time ago. She went out to the street and told the neighbor that she and the old lady were off to the olive grove, and that if anyone came by, to say no one was home. Then, just as before, she locked the door, with her mother-in-law watching, puzzled. But

Beleta indicated that she should follow her to the kneading room, and once inside, armed with her father-in-law's tool, she removed the coal basket that was always in the back corner and started to take the stones out of the floor. She didn't have to be quite so careful now, since the old man had died some months earlier and no one was around to accuse her of violating secrets as long as she discreetly covered them up.

Her mother-in-law couldn't believe her eyes. Scratching away, Beleta uncovered the lid and then the jar; she took out the bran by handfuls, then the old sock, stuffed like a sausage. Behind that, she took out a red cotton pouch, divided between *napoleons* and bars of coins (this part was new for Beleta; she had kept an eye on the hiding place as best she could, but she hadn't seen her father-in-law poking around there since that first time). She stopped suddenly.

When the old lady saw that pile of silver coins stuffed into the lid, she nearly fainted, and when Beleta lovingly put the palm basket into her hands, she turned as white as the wall and a great sob of joy burst forth from her throat.

"Good heavens! My dowry! I never saw it again since they set it in front of me at the wedding banquet!" She clutched the basket against her chest, deeply moved. After a moment, she added with painful resentment: "He made me suffer so much, and save, even to skimp on food! He said we were poor, that we'd lost lots of money in the business!"

Another surprise: she asked the young woman, "But how did you know about all this, my dear?"

And Beleta explained, ending her story: "But since the secret belonged not to me—you know?—but to your husband, I said nothing to anyone. I didn't think it was right to get involved."

"So now, no one knows about it?"

"Not a soul."

"But, you mean all this is mine? What do you think I should do now, Beleta?"

"Nothing. It's all yours. It's your right, and your savings. Keep it for yourself."

"But what about your husband?"

"We're still young, and we're earning a living, thank God. And if you die before we do and there's anything left, we'll find it. Meantime, you might need it, like now, to help out your young daughter."

"You're right, my poor little girl! To think we should be afflicted with such a disgrace! Of all the unhappiness I've seen, this one has hurt me most. It's lucky for me I have you on my side, Bel!"

"You've always been good to me, too. And as the saying goes, 'Reap what you sow,' " she responded modestly.

The two of them decided not to tell anyone, and they put the hiding place back together as best they could, leaving the jar of bran in its place, *in case they might need it again another day.* The old lady wanted her daughter-in-law to help her take the treasure upstairs to hide it again (Beleta advised this) in the bottom of an old drawer, so old it was falling apart; a place no one ever poked around in since it held only absolutely useless things: a damask jacket that had belonged to one of the old lady's rich great-grandmothers, corseted in esparto; a little baptismal gown from the last century with its ribbons all stained, moldy, and fragile as paper; baby books of the old uncle who never married; Papal Bulls from the Crusades, yellow as chickpeas, moth-eaten, with the letters as grainy as fleas; her son's first rattle; the little tobacco box and clogs from the other great-grandfather, who had built the house; bits of candle still bearing strips of variegated colored paper, left over every year from Holy Week and only used to light up the ceremony when they entered the house of the Lord if some family member was seriously ill; and other similar relics that had no interest at all for young people but that the mother-in-law zealously guarded. Now those things would be joined by another relic, the most valuable of all, the basket of palm leaves.

And so the young sister-in-law went up to the mountain to help Beleta's sister in her healthy and solitary farmhouse. A few months later, after having delivered a stillborn baby, she came home. She was as fine and serious as ever, even fresher and prettier than before, with her face like a rose and with a confident attitude. A fellow from a nearby village, a friend of her brother, fell in love with her at first sight, and they were soon married. The groom was well established, and she made a good match. The soldier had gone off to Mallorca, where his wife lived, before the girl returned. The young sister-in-law became the mother of four children, and her husband bought new fields every year. Her brother was convinced that she owed him that good fortune, for having allowed her to go spend time with Beleta's sick sister, and everyone went along with that idea since no one wanted to contradict anything he said.

Distracted by those memories that brought scenes of the past to life, just as if they were before her eyes now, a little tired and sweaty, Beleta kneaded mechanically, tearing off pieces of the dough and then putting them back, beating them forcefully against the trough, sprinkling more flour and repeating the exercise, folding it over and rubbing it without stopping. The mound grew and grew, more and more. By now it was hard for her to lift it against her chest to turn it over; it was expanding everywhere, and it was heavy, too; she could barely pick it up. No wonder it left her arms sore and her kidneys aching. It would be days before she could stretch out straight, but she continued her struggle, like an obsession let loose, her imagination absorbed by the images she had seen within those *blessed* walls during the years she had been there. Seen almost by fraud, or by chance, or thanks to the bewitching shadows that at certain hours hid everything to those who were just coming in out of the light, like that other time . . .

Now she could see her mother-in-law as if she had her right there. Thinking she was alone, the old lady inspected the inside of a jacket with great attention beneath the slanting ray of light coming in through the window, cut in half by the iron bar. Then she straddled the jacket on the chair back and took out the inside, searching and examining. She didn't have to look far, because that stain, the trail of suppuration from the wound, stood out clearly. Suddenly Beleta understood certain things she had tucked away in her subconscious, things she thought were odd but couldn't quite figure out: her mother-in-law's frequent trips to the basin, where she splashed herself, half hidden; it was always the same basin, and she didn't want anyone else to touch it; not wanting to wash her clothes with the clothes of others; the weakness of her left arm when she picked up the basket or folded sheets . . . Beleta understood: her mother-in-law had some disease, and to judge by the precautions she took, it was a very serious one. In fact, a grave one indeed. One day her mother-in-law had gone to market in the next village, alone, and she had talked to a doctor. He had spoken plainly. Beleta was deeply moved by an immense pity, and she came out of the dark: her mother-in-law had a terrible scare and turned white as wax.

"But why didn't you tell us, for heaven's sake! Shared troubles are easier to bear!" exclaimed Beleta.

"Diseases are so disgusting, I didn't want to be repulsive to everybody," she confessed, afraid and ashamed.

"But going through a thing like that all alone!" Beleta murmured with great pain and sorrow.

From that day on, Beleta behaved as a dutiful daughter; not satisfied with the diagnosis of the first doctor, she took her to one after another. Unfortunately, the disease had advanced so that no cure was possible. At that point, Beleta spoke to her husband and her two sisters-in-law so that everyone would be alerted to what might happen from one moment to the next. But God had mercy on them all and took the old lady, victim of a bout of bronchopneumonia; it didn't last long. Beleta became the lady of the house, but that was cold comfort. She had lost her own mother as a baby, and she had always loved her mother-in-law as if she were really her mother; she never minded living under the old lady's authority . . . "for she was a discreet and considerate woman by nature . . . not at all like the others . . . Oh, if the others had been like her, good lord, things would have been very different in the house I grew to love. But . . ."

The blows and kneading of the dough came on faster, and seemed in tune with Beleta's reveries as she hit the big mound against the trough once and again. She went further back in time.

"If they had all been more like her. That's why my mother-in-law's death was the cruelest blow, and she had been through all kinds of suffering."

Finally, the exhausted baker decided to make partitions, and she set each inflated, round ball in its proper basket, arranging them on the plank. How many loaves were there? Four, five, six . . . Six: she thought there would be more, but they were big, bah! It was fine, why eat stale bread when you could eat it fresh? They would disappear soon enough.

As she scrubbed trough and tools and put each item in its place, the *catric, catrac* of her thinking went back along those paths, resuscitating that last retrospective image vividly against the turbid background.

She had got up at daybreak that day to straighten up the house, get the drinks ready for the men, take it all out to the field where they were reaping, come back home and cook dinner, go back to the field, wash that mountain of vessels . . . She was weary, and it was so hot that day.

She went into the kneading room, took the low chair, and, untying her jacket to mid-chest, sat down in the same dark corner she always did, between the winch and the wall, to calm down and rest a bit. But she rested so well, she dozed off without realizing it. She dreamed: she dreamed that the reaping machine was making an odd noise, a *rum-rum* different from before, as if it were talking, like a person. It was the talking that bothered her sleep and in the end woke her up. She opened her eyes slowly. "No, it wasn't a machine that was talking, it was a man . . . my husband . . . but wasn't he in the fields with the workers?" A bit of consciousness brought her back . . . Yes, yes, it was her husband . . . how strange! Why did he come back in? Perhaps the sun was too much . . . he had complained about a headache. She wanted to ask him, but she didn't have the strength . . . then she heard another voice, a low, pleading voice. "Someone else was there too. Who could it be?" She was now completely awake. No doubt another person was there, a woman, it was the neighbor from across the street . . . but what on earth were they saying?

"Times are bad, Carme, I have the expenses of reaping, and I'm just about broke, too broke . . . and what work will they do if I'm not there? It's lucky she's vigilant . . . but I shouldn't have come, really, it's just that last night you looked so depressed."

"I didn't have a chance to tell you. He has gambled everything away, and I don't have a cent in the house."

A flash of rancor and rage passed over his face: "You're the one who wanted that! Why did you marry him? You knew what he was like!"

"Mother made me do it . . . I didn't want him," she said, her voice cajoling. "I liked you better."

"Nonsense, Carme!" He jumped in, full of spite. "You had no trouble turning me down!"

"If you had waited, maybe . . . but you got married right away!"

"What was I supposed to do? Fall into more rage, watching him shuffling around all the time?"

"No, no, don't say that." A slightly accusatory tone. "You were keen on her from the beginning."

He spat out quickly: "Keen? Don't make me laugh!"

"You always said you didn't like the dry type!"

"And I still say it. I'll say it again!"

"Then why?"

"Because I wanted to marry right away, before you had a chance to, and she was the first one to cross my path, that's why! Now you know." Suddenly, in his typically harsh tone, he spat out: "Okay, I've got to get back." Then, as if in coordination with what he had told his wife that morning, he said: "I told her I didn't feel well and that I might come to get some medicinal water, but if I delay any more, I could run into her on the way back."

The neighbor from across the street replied in a cold, calculating voice: "All right then, but what about the other matter?"

"Oh, I had forgotten," and he checked out his pants pockets. "Here, take a few bucks, at the moment it's all I can give you."

She moved her head enigmatically, and he went to the door, looking up and down the street. He turned back into the kneading room and said, "Come on, leave after me. Since she's out of the house, it's better if people don't see us; it could get back to her."

Overwhelmed, incapable of getting out of the chair, Beleta watched them go. When she was finally able to move, her arms hung down with strange lassitude the length of her trunk, and her legs would not obey her wishes. She had aged twenty years, and from that day forward she would never be the same. Still, after long periods of quiet dejection, that last unhappy vision began to make its way into the background as well, like all things that are not in a hurry. The image faded into space, just as a caravan going across the fields gets foggy and finally blurs into the deserts of equivocal sleep.

Beleta shook her head with heroic resolution, tired of disappointments and sacrifices. Then she glanced around with a vague look, and when she saw that row of loaves on the shelf, turgid and hard like a woman's breasts, created by her hands and emanating her warmth, a soothing voluptuousness came to comfort her. She was aware that for good or evil, or perhaps for good and evil, everything alive inside her was tied to that kneading room. In the shadowy and mysterious room, sacristy of such strange goings-on, in which she had spent such long hours and had heard, without intending to, so many words; she had witnessed so many actions that would become source and object of the most poignant reactions that at times jolt the miserable human heart.

PARTS IN A PLAY

After saying good afternoon, Mr. Anton sat on the stones next to the rim of the well and watched Pelegrí as he worked, closing up the head of a saturated furrow and opening the next one with his hoe until he had watered the whole field. Anton said with a little irony in his voice: "Yesterday I went by your house, and I was going to ask if you were coming today, but I heard you yelling and screaming, so I thought better of it and kept on going."

Pelegrí answered in a normal tone, pulling up his pants, which had slipped down: "I was arguing with my wife."

"Oh, yeah, I figured that. Like every day, right? Except that, to argue, you need two, and I only heard your voice."

"She was upstairs in the kitchen."

"Don't give me that, Pelegrí. The fact is that she didn't say anything; you have a bad temper, if you don't mind my saying so."

"Mr. Anton, women are a kind of beast that you have to lead along very carefully if you want them to work right."

"Women, Pelegrí, are just like you and me, more or less, and if we want to be respected, we have to respect them too, especially our wives, who are men's best helpers."

Pelegrí straightened up, his mouth closed, lips pulled toward the right cheek; it was his characteristic smile.

"What can I say, Mr. Anton," he replied skeptically, with a mocking laugh. "A woman is always a woman, and a man is always a man."

Mr. Anton answered seriously: "If one of these days she gets tired of you and your abuse and takes off, then we'll see what you have to say."

At that moment, Mr. Anton's dog, Linda, started scratching at one of the furrows and broke the ridge open. Pelegrí swung at her with his hoe and repaired the damage, yelling at the dog's owner; the terrified dog ran to crouch between Anton's legs. The thoughts of both men turned back to the job, and they dropped their conversation. The topic was so common among all the townspeople that they didn't talk about it much anymore.

For Pelegrí's vile temper was an everyday thing: he had taken up abusive language as his favorite sport, using more serious abuse on his poor wife, a good person, prudent and hardworking, who always had, as everyone said, her soul hanging from a thread.

The neighbors knew what was coming every day when darkness came and he returned home from work. As soon as he opened the outside door, before entering the courtyard to bring the mule in, he would start his complaining with whatever pretext, or with none at all, and the storm would break out soon afterward.

Knowing the impending danger, Maria, working in the kitchen at that hour, started sweating buckets as soon as she heard the street door squeaking, for she knew all too well just what awaited her: as soon as Pelegrí stuck his nose in at the top of the stair, he would grab whatever was at hand, a stick, a chair, the staff . . . until one day he caught the cat by the tail and tried to throw it at his wife. But the cat turned around like a bad spirit and, among shrieking meows, clawed deeply into his hands and fled from him like lightning. The next day the cat got an implacable beating, but Pelegrí's hand didn't fare well either; it was striped like a road map with red lines all over. The incident was the topic of the neighborhood, and one of the women said to Maria:

"It's unbelievable how a strong woman like yourself doesn't have the courage to fight back like the cat did. It's not going to make things worse for the cat."

Another added: "Can't you see he's doing all that for his own fun?"

A third one added mockingly: "He takes it out on you, and that calms him down."

Things went on like that for eight or ten years: he yelling and beating her nearly every day, and she always with a lump in her throat, fearful; her inner trembling caused her to break quite a few plates at dinnertime (for that's when those things usually took place, in the evenings). Her shoulders got more and more bent over, like a poor creature abandoned by God.

Until one time . . .

It was the season to bring in the year's wheat to be ground for bread. Pelegrí had asked for his time first thing the next morning. Since he wasn't lazy, he decided that before taking things over to Mr. Anton's orchard, he could get everything all ready for the next day.

He had the cart in the courtyard next door and the sack of wheat at the entrance to the house. If he put the sack in the cart now and brought it through the interior door to the courtyard, he wouldn't have to grunt and groan on the street the next day, giving the neighbors something to talk about. Pelegrí was well aware that he wasn't very popular with them, and as far as he was concerned, they were all a bunch of gossips full of envy. So he took the sack by its ties and tried to lift it up in the air, but the sack was large and very heavy, as if it contained iron instead of wheat.

He tried again and again. Sweat was pouring down his face as if he had it under a spigot; his temples beat as if they would explode; he was huffing and puffing like a bellows, his back was giving out, the muscles of his belly were painfully tense; but no matter how much he struggled, he couldn't make it budge. He managed to get it off the ground enough to drag it from one side to the other, but he couldn't get it any higher. Enraged with himself, his temper at breaking point, he let it go and gave the sack half a dozen kicks, harder than the ones he gave the mule when she wouldn't move.

"Damn it all! It's all worthless! I must be getting weak!" After a moment of indecision, scratching the dried-up hair on his scalp with stubby fingernails, he concluded: "No way around it, I'm going to have to divide it into two sacks. I don't want everybody at the mill to make fun of me, seeing me struggle with the damn thing."

From up in the kitchen, Maria carefully watched the scene with great interest.

When he left the house for Mr. Anton's orchard, she came downstairs, bolted the door so no one could surprise her, and took her turn at lifting up the sack of wheat. She couldn't do it; the sack was completely immobile on the ground, like a tree.

Hands together and gaze fixed as if offering up a mental prayer, the woman mulled it over. Clearly, she wouldn't get anywhere that way. She looked around. In a corner of the entryway was the tub for making wine, half hidden in the ground, half sticking up along wall, about four hand-lengths high. Solid oak, licorice-colored posts covered the wide, circular opening. Maria took one of the posts and stuck it along the ground at the edge of the tub, like a little diagonal bridge. Then, very slowly, patiently, and skillfully, she pushed it back and forth, one end and then the other, making the imposing bulk move along, until she got it to the foot of the post, where she left it lying on the edge. She went to the courtyard and got the reins of the mule, tying them around the middle of the sack. Then, jumping up on top of the tub, she wrapped the reins around her hands, propped up her legs, stiff as scaffold bars, and started to pull the cord, "hala, hala, hala, hala," until the sack moved, and then, with insecure jerks, she began to drag it along the incline. But no letting up—if she loosened at all, the sack would not only slip back down but also maybe take her with it. Her stubbornness won the day, for the sack was hoisted up to the end of the wood and brought to the edge of pebbles covering the wall. Exhausted and satisfied, she smiled, breathing deeply. When she felt rested, she jumped down from the tub, put her back to the wall and grabbed the strings of the sack, tilting it until it was on her back. At that point, she thought the whole house had fallen on top of her; the blow was so terrible that she lost sight of the world, her legs shook, and she just about fell over with the thing on top of her. She didn't give up. She mustered up all her forces, closed her trembling legs, straightened up her trunk little by little, took two shaky steps, and bent over, nearly in half, she turned around to the entry with the sack of wheat on her back. When she got to the point where her husband had left it, Maria let it go. Her chest was huffing like a bellows, she saw stars and wasn't sure whether she was still in this world or in the other, but she had succeeded in her task. Now she knew she was stronger than Pelegrí, stronger and smarter.

That evening, as soon as she heard him come in, she went to the stairway and yelled out at him in the harshest of tones: "Shut the damn door, if you don't mind! With the wind blowing, the chimney won't draw, and I'm getting all the smoke!"

His mouth dropped in astonishment as he set his foot on the first step: Was that his Maria speaking? He bounded violently up the stair, furious, but before he got to the kitchen, a huge head of cabbage, hurled as if in a comic battle, smacked him in the middle of the face, and he nearly fell back down the stairs. Another moment of stupefaction: he started up again. He didn't make it; his wife, with feet firmly planted on the ground, waited serenely with pitchfork in hand, looking most resolute. He stopped short. She repeated, calm but firm: "I told you that the chimney isn't drawing. Go get the door!"

Pelegrí hesitated for a second, but what did he discern, something secretly threatening, in his wife's tone, in her fiery stare, that made all his meanness melt away like ice in a furnace? He paused again, just for a moment, and finally, bitterly amazed, he bowed his head, turned around, and step by step, as if each movement took an immense effort, he went down and took care of the door.

That was the first chapter, or the prologue, of a new life. From that evening on, Maria treated her husband exactly as he had treated her up to now. Every day when he returned from work, rightly or wrongly, he was greeted with a scolding.

"How come you're so late? Did you stop along the way to make puppets? What took you so long?"

"I went to take the tools back."

She answered with a mocking laugh: "I'm sure the smithy is delighted to have you show up just when it's quitting time."

"Won't you ever finish putting things away? For the racket you make, anyone would think there was a regiment of soldiers here!"

Or, raising her eyes to the heavens: "God give me patience to put up with a fool like you! I've been telling you for three days not to get in my way at the fireplace, are you deaf or something?"

And so it went, day after day, if he didn't find the broom tossed at his head, the old pruner landed at his feet with great risk of bodily harm.

He tried desperately one day to go back to the way things were, but as soon as she saw him come near, she tripped him and was on top of him, slapping his face again and again. She said in a tone that admitted no reply: "If you ever try those games with me again, you're going to be sorry. I swear it!"

He heard that, and since he could never figure out where all that strange miracle in reverse was coming from, because Maria hadn't explained a thing to him or anyone else, all he could do was repeat into his own hat over and over again with manic tenacity: "They've put a spell on her! Someone has put a spell on her!"

And since he was convinced that what had happened was something unnatural, from the power of Hades, which man could do nothing about, his load became lighter and his destiny easier to accept.

People have ears, and from street to street it didn't take long for the whole town to see what the new situation was. The ladies gossiped, the young men at the tavern and the workers spoke of nothing else. Laughter was general, and the comments more stinging than insect bites. That lasted until, as time went by, the novelty wore off and the caustic remarks lost their virulence. The story got old in the town's repertoire.

And so, one day Mr. Anton and Pelegrí ran into each other in the orchard, one seated on the stones at the edge of the well and the other closing the water to a furrow of soaked tomatoes and opening up another with a swift blow of his hoe. Again, Mr. Anton, with a roguish gleam in his old gaze, took the old subject up once more: "What's that bruise you have on your forehead, Pelegrí?"

Pelegrí hung his head down with resignation and answered straight to the point, sure that Mr. Anton and everyone else in town knew exactly what was going on: "Well, you can just imagine! What can I tell you? It's an unfortunate man in this life who gets involved with a bad beast!"

But that time he didn't pull his cheek to the edge of his mouth, for it had been a long time since he had lost his characteristic grimace of a mocking laugh.